CHAPTER ONE

CHRISTMAS. It was *that* time of year again. Not in a jolly mood, Vito Barbieri grimaced, his darkly handsome features hard with impatience. He had no time for it—the silliness of the festive season, the drunken antics and the extravagance, not to mention the lack of concentration, increased absenteeism and reduced productivity from his thousands of staff. January was never a good month for the profit margins.

Nor was he ever likely to forget the Christmas when he had lost his kid brother, Olly. Although three years had passed the tragedy of Olly's horribly wasted life was still etched on his mind. His little brother, so bright and full of promise, had died because a drunk got behind a car wheel after a party, Vito's party, where he and his brother had argued minutes before that fatal car journey. Guilt clouded his happier memories of the boy, ten years his junior, whom he had loved above all else.

But then love always *hurt*. Vito had learned that lesson young when his mother walked out on her husband and son for a much richer man. He never saw her again. His father had neglected him and rushed into a series of fleeting affairs. Olly had been the result of one of those affairs, orphaned at nine years old when his English mother died. Vito had offered him a home. It was probably the only act of generosity Vito had never regretted, for, much as he missed Olly, he was still grateful to have known him. His sibling's sunny outlook had briefly enriched Vito's workaholic existence.

Only now Bolderwood Castle, purchased purely because Olly fancied living in a gothic monstrosity complete with turrets, was no longer a home. Of course he could take a wife and watch her walk away with half his fortune, his castle and his children, a lesson so many of his friends had learned to their cost, a few years down the road. No, there would be no wife, Vito reflected grimly. When a man was as rich as Vito, greedy, ambitious women literally threw themselves at his feet. But tall or short, curvy or skinny, dark or fair, the women who met the needs of his high sex drive were virtually interchangeable. Indeed sex was steadily becoming nothing to get excited about, he acknowledged wryly. At thirty-one years of age, Vito was reviewing the attributes he used to define an attractive woman by.

He knew what he *didn't* like. Airheads irritated him. He was not a patient or tolerant man. Intellectual snobs, party girls and social climbers bored him. Giggly, flirtatious ones reminded him too much of his misspent youth and tough career women rarely knew how to lighten up at the end of the day. Either that or they wanted a four point plan of any relationship laid out in advance. Did he want children? Did he actually know if he was fertile? Did he want to settle down some day? No, he didn't. He wasn't opening himself up to that level of disillusionment; particularly not after losing Olly had taught him how transitory life could be. He would be a very rich and cantankerous and demanding old man instead.

There was a knock on the door and a woman entered the room. Karen Harper, his office manager, Vito recalled after a momentary pause; AeroCarlton, which manufactured aeroplane parts, was a recent acquisition in Vito's business empire and he was only just getting to know the staff.

'I'm sorry to disturb you, Mr Barbieri. I wanted to check that you're happy to continue endorsing the prisoner rehabilitation placement scheme we joined last year? It's run by the charity New Start and they recommend suitable applicants who they fully check out and support. We have an office trainee starting tomorrow. Her name's—'

'I don't need to know the details,' Vito cut in smoothly, 'I have no objection to operating such a scheme but will expect you to keep a close watch on the employee.'

'Of course,' the attractive brunette declared with a bright smile of approval. 'It feels good at this time of year to give someone in difficulty a new chance in life, doesn't it? And the placement does only last three months.'

More goody-goody sentimental drivel, Vito thought in exasperation. He supposed the applicant had paid her debt to society through serving her sentence in prison but he was not particularly enamoured of the prospect of having a potential villain on the premises. 'Did this person's crime involve dishonesty?' he queried suddenly.

'No, we were clear that we wouldn't accept anyone with that kind of record. I doubt if you'll even see her, Mr Barbieri. She'll be the office gopher. She can take care of messages, filing and man reception. At this time of year, there's always room for an extra pair of hands.'

A momentary pang of conscience assailed Vito, for,

astute as he was, he had already noticed that the manager could be a little too tough on her subordinates. Only the day before he had overheard her taking the janitor to task over a very minor infringement of his duties. Karen enjoyed her position of power and used it, but he could only assume that an ex-con would be well equipped to cope.

Ava checked the postbox as she did at least twice every day. Nothing. There was no point trying to avoid the obvious, no point in continuing to hope—her family wanted nothing more to do with her and had decided to ignore her letters. Tears pricked her bright blue eyes and she blinked rapidly, lifting her coppery head high. She had learned to get by on her own in prison and she could do the same in the outside world, even if the outside world was filled with a bewildering array of choices, disappointments and possibilities that made her head swim.

'Don't try to run before you can walk,' her probation officer had advised. Sally was a great believer in platitudes.

Harvey's tail thumped the floor at Ava's feet and she bent down to smooth his soft curly head. A cross between a German shepherd and a poodle, Harvey was a large dog with floppy ears, a thick black curly coat and a long shaggy tail that looked as though it belonged to another breed entirely.

'Time to get you home, boy,' Ava said softly, trying not to think about the fact that the boarding kennels where Harvey lived could not possibly house him for much longer. During the last few months of her sentence Ava worked at the kennels—outside work was encouraged as a means of reintroducing prisoners into the community and independent life—and she was all too well aware that Harvey was living on borrowed time.

She loved Harvey with all her heart and soul. He was the one thing in her life that she dared love now, and on the days she saw him he lifted her heart as nothing else could. But Marge, the kind lady who ran the kennels and took in strays, had limited space and Harvey had already spent months in her care without finding a home. Harvey, however, was his own worst enemy because he barked at the people who might have given him a for-ever home, scaring them off before they could learn about his gentle, loyal character and clean habits. Ava knew how big the gap between appearances and reality could be; she had spent so many years putting on a false front to keep people at arm's length, believing that she didn't need anyone, didn't care about other people's opinions and was proud to be the odd one out. At home, at school, just about everywhere she went, Ava had been alone…

Except for Olly, she thought, and a fierce pang of pain and regret shot through her as sharply as a knife. Oliver Barbieri had been her best friend and she had to live with the knowledge that it was her fault he was dead. She had gone to prison for reckless driving but the memory of the trial was blurred because she had already been living in a mental hell and no court could have punished her more than she had punished herself. It hadn't mattered that her father had thrown her out of the house in disgust or even that she had been advised not to attend Olly's funeral and pay her last respects. She had known she didn't deserve pity or forgiveness. Even so she did not remember the crash. During it she had sustained a head injury and was left with memory loss, meaning she recalled neither her fateful, incomprehensible decision to drive while under the influence of alcohol or the accident itself. Sometimes she thought that amnesia was a blessing, and sometimes that only fear of reliving what she had done lay behind her inability to recall the later stages of that awful night.

She had met Olly at boarding school, a trendy co-ed institution with high fees and a fantastic academic record. No price had been too high for her father to get his least-loved child out from under his roof, she acknowledged sadly. Always made to feel like the cuckoo in the family nest, Ava was the only one of three children to have been sent away from home to receive her education. It had driven yet another wedge between Ava and her sisters, Gina and Bella, and, now that she had truly become the prodigal daughter, there was no sign that anyone wanted to welcome her back to the fold. Of course her mother was dead and there was nobody left to mend fences or at least nobody who cared enough to make the effort. Her sisters had their own lives with husbands and children and careers and their ex-con sister was simply an embarrassment, a stain on the Fitzgerald family name.

Scolding herself for that demoralising flood of negative reflections, Ava strove instead to concentrate on the positives: she was out of prison, she had a job, an actual *job*—she still couldn't believe her good fortune. When she had first been recommended for the New Start programme she had not held out much hope of a placement because, although she had left school with top grades, she had no relevant office work experience or saleable skills. But AeroCarlton had offered her a lifebelt, giving her the chance to rebuild her life, with a reputable firm on her CV she would have a much better chance of getting a permanent job.

Harvey's tail dropped as he stepped through the doors of his foster home. Marge put on the kettle and shooed him out into the garden because he took up too much space indoors. Marooned there, Harvey pressed his nose to the glass of the French windows in the living room, watching Ava's every move.

'Here…pass this around tomorrow when you start your new job,' Marge urged, pressing a paper catalogue on Ava. 'A few orders would be very welcome and I've got to say that the work my lovely ladies have put in so far is exceptional.'

Ava glanced through the booklet of hand-knit and embroidered cushions, bookmarks, hat and scarf sets; spectacle cases, toys and even lavender bags, most of which depicted various cat and dog breeds. In an effort to raise money to fund the stray and abandoned animals currently staying in her kennels, as well as in local foster homes, Marge had set up a little cottage industry of animal-loving neighbours and supporters who knit and sewed. It was an impressive display of merchandise, nicely timed for the Christmas market, but, Ava thought ruefully, the ladies could have broadened their designs a little to appeal more to the younger market.

'I know you walked here for Harvey's benefit but have you got your bus fare home?' Marge pressed anxiously, her friendly face troubled by the tiredness etched in Ava's delicate features.

'Of course I have,' Ava lied, not wanting Marge to put her hand into her own far from deep purse.

'And have you got a decent outfit to wear tomorrow?' Marge checked. 'You'll have to dress smart for a big office.'

'I picked up a trouser suit in a charity shop.' Ava would not have dreamt of admitting that the trousers were a little too tight and the jacket unable to button over her rather too generous bust. Wearing them with a blue shirt, she would look smart enough and nobody was likely to notice that her flat black shoes were too big. She would have liked shoes with a heel but beggars couldn't be choosers and it would take a lot of paydays to build up a working wardrobe. Once she had adored fashion, but she had given up that pursuit along with so many other interests that were no longer appropriate. Now she concentrated on the far more important challenge of simply getting by, which came down to paying rent, feeding and clothing herself as best she could. The adventurous, defiant girl who had sported the Goth look—black lace, leather and dyed black hair cut short as a boy's—had died along with Olly in that car crash, she conceded painfully, barely recognising the very cautious and sensible young woman she had become.

Prison had taught her to seek anonymity. Standing out from the crowd there would have been dangerous. She had learned to keep her head down, follow the rules, help out when she could, keep her mouth shut when she couldn't. Prison had shamed her, just as the judgement of the court had shamed her. Much had been made of her fall in the local newspaper because of her comfortable family background and private school education. At the time she had thought it very unfair that she should be pilloried for what she could not help. Then in prison she had met women who could barely read, write or count and she had worked with them, recognising their more basic problems. For them, getting involved in criminal activities had only been a means of survival, and Ava knew that she had never had that excuse.

So what if your father never liked you? So what if your mother never defended you or hugged you and both parents always favoured your sisters over you? So what if they labelled you a troublemaker in primary school where you got bullied? So what if your mother was an alcoholic and her problems were ignored for years?

There would never be an excuse for what she had done to Olly, whom she had loved like a brother, she thought wretchedly as she walked wearily home to her bedsit. Everything always seemed to come back round to the events of that dreadful night. But somehow she had to learn to live with her massive mistake and move on from it. She would never ever forget her best friend but she knew he would have been the first to tell her to stop tormenting herself. Olly had always been wonderfully practical and great at cutting through all the superficial stuff to the heart of a problem. Had he lived, he would have become a wonderful doctor.

'It's not your fault that your mother drinks…it's not your fault that your parents' marriage is falling apart or that your sisters are spoiled stuck-up little brats! Why do you always take on the blame for everything wrong in your family?' Olly used to demand impatiently.

Full of anticipation, Ava laid out her clothes for the next morning. Having been assured by New Start that her history would remain confidential, she had no fear of being seen as anything other than the new office junior. She had learned to love being busy and useful because that gave her a feeling of achievement, instead of the hollow sense of self-loathing that had haunted her for months after the crash when she had had far too many idle hours in which to dwell on her mistakes.

'You can make the coffee for the meeting. There will be twenty members of staff attending,' Karen Harper pronounced with a steely smile. 'You can make coffee?'

Ava nodded vigorously, willing to do anything to please and already sensing that pleasing Miss Harper, as she had introduced herself, might be a challenge. Shown into the small kitchen, she checked out where everything was and got busy.

At ten forty-five, Ava wheeled the trolley into the conference room where a formidably tall man was speaking to the staff surrounding the long table. There was colossal tension in the room and nobody else spoke at all. He was talking about change being inevitable but…it would not be happening overnight and redundancies looked unlikely. His voice had a mellifluous accent that was instantly recognisable and familiar to her ears: Italian. As his audience shifted in their seats with collective relief at the forecast, Ava poured the boss's coffee with a shaking hand. Black, two sugars, according to the list. It could *not* be Vito, her dazed mind was telling her, it could not possibly be Vito. Fate could not have served her up a job in a company run by the man whom she had most injured. And yet she *knew* Vito's voice, the deep drawl laced with a lilt over certain vowel sounds that used to make her tummy flip as if she were on a roller coaster. She did not dare look, would not allow herself to look, as she walked down the side of the room to serve the boss first and slipped right out of her too large shoes so that by the time she reached the top of the table she was barefoot!

Vito had glanced at the girl bent over the coffee trolley, noting the fiery hair glinting with gold and copper highlights wound into a knot on the top of her head, the delicacy of her profile, the elegance of her slender white hands and the tight fit of her trousers over the small curvy behind that segued down into long slim legs. There was something about her, something that captured his attention, something maddeningly familiar but what it was he could not have said until she straightened and he saw an elfin face dominated by pansy blue eyes. His breath caught in his lungs and he stopped breathing, unable to believe that it could be *her.* The last time he had seen her she had had black hair cropped short and the blank look of trauma in her gaze as if she couldn't see or hear anything happening around her. Ferocious tension etched harsh lines into the almost feral beauty of his strong handsome face.

Oh dear heaven, it was Vito Barbieri! Feeling sick from shock, Ava froze with his cup of coffee rattling in her trembling hand.

'Thank you,' Vito breathed with no expression at all, his dark golden eyes skimming her pale shaken visage as he accepted the coffee from her.

'Mr Barbieri, this is Ava Fitzgerald who joined the staff today,' Karen Harper advanced helpfully.

'We've already met,' Vito pronounced with icy bite. 'Come back when the meeting is over, Ava. I'd like to speak to you.'

Ava managed to step smoothly back into her shoes on her way back to the tea trolley. With the rigorous self-discipline she had picked up in prison, she served the rest of the coffee without mishap although her skin was clammy with perspiration and she breathed in and out rapidly to get a grip on herself.

Vito Barbieri—it was a horrible coincidence that her job opportunity should turn out to be in his business. But what on earth was he doing at AeroCarlton? She had read the company website and there had been no reference to Vito, yet he was obviously the boss. So much for her big break! Vito wouldn't want her anywhere near him: he despised her. When she returned to that room he would tell her that she was sacked. Of course he would. What else could she expect him to do? It was her fault that Olly was dead so why would he employ her? He had been shocked to see her. The grim tightness of those lean, bronzed features had been unusually revealing. Had he known who she was in advance he would have withdrawn her placement before she'd even arrived at AeroCarlton.

Vito, the bane of her life from the age of sixteen. She clamped an uneasy hand to the tattoo seared over her left hip where it seemed to burn like a brand. She had been such a stupid and impulsive teenager, she acknowledged wretchedly, deeply shaken by the encounter that had just taken place. None of the boys at school had attracted her. She had had to go home with Olly for the weekend to see her dream guy. Ten years her senior and a fully grown adult male with the killer instincts of a business shark, her dream guy had barely noticed she was alive, let alone sitting up and begging for his attention. True, he had seemed a little taken aback by his brother's choice of companion, taking in Ava in her Goth getup with her dyed black hair and mutinous expression. She had never stayed in a castle before and had been trying very hard to act as if she were cool with the intimidating experience.

'Ava?' Ava wheeled round and found Karen Harper studying her. 'You didn't mention that you knew Mr Barbieri...'

'My father works for him and we lived near his home,' Ava admitted awkwardly.

The brunette pursed her lips. 'Well, don't expect that to cut you any slack,' she warned. 'Mr Barbieri's waiting for you. Clear the coffee cups while you're in there.'

'Yes. I didn't know he...er...worked here.'

'Mr Barbieri took over AeroCarlton last week. He's your employer.'

'Right...' With a polite smile that was wasted on the disgruntled woman frowning at her, Ava beat a swift retreat, nausea bubbling in the pit of her stomach. Serious bad luck seemed to follow her round like a nasty shadow! Here she was trying to adjust to being back in the world again and the one man who probably wished that the authorities had kept her locked up turned out to be her new boss.

Vito was resting back against the edge of the table and talking on the phone in fast fluid Italian when she reappeared. Nervous as a cat facing a lion, Ava used the time to quietly load the china back onto the trolley but the image of him remained welded onto her eyelids: the tailored black business suit cut to precision on his very tall, broad shouldered and lean-hipped frame, the white shirt so crisp against his bronzed skin, the gold silk tie that echoed his eyes in sunlight. He was breathtakingly good-looking and exotic from the bold thrust of his high cheekbones and strong nose to his slashing dark brows and beautifully moulded sensual mouth.

He hadn't changed. He still exuded an aura of authority and crackling energy that whipped up a tension all of its own. Olly's big brother, she thought painfully, and if only she had listened to Olly her best friend might still have been alive.

'Stop trying to flirt with Vito, stop throwing yourself at him!' Olly had warned her in exasperation the night of that fatal party. 'You're not his type and you're too young for him and even if you weren't, Vito would eat you for breakfast. He's a predator with women.'

Back then Vito's type had been sleek, blonde, elegant and sophisticated, everything Ava was not, and the comparison had torn her up. He had been out of reach; so far above her it had broken her heart. She had become obsessed by Vito Barbieri, wildly infatuated as only a stubborn lovelorn teenager could be, cherishing every little scrap of information she could find out about him. He took sugar in his coffee and he liked chocolate. He supported several children's charities that dispensed medical aid in developing countries. He had suffered a challenging childhood when his parents broke up and his father took to alcohol and other women to assuage his grief. He loved to drive fast and collected cars. Although he had perfect teeth he hated going to the dentist. The recollection of all those once very much prized little facts sank Ava dangerously deep into the clinging tentacles of the past she had buried.

'We'll talk in my office next door,' Vito decreed, having come off the phone. He moved away from the table and opened a door on the other side of the room. 'Leave the damn trolley!'

That impatient exclamation made her hand shoot back from the handle she had automatically been reaching for. Colour ran like a rising flag up her slender throat into her heart-shaped face, flushing her cheeks with discomfiture.

Stunning eyes narrowed, Vito studied her, his attention descending from the multicoloured topknot that was so unfamiliar to him, down over her pale perfect face with those big blue eyes, that dainty little nose and lush, incredibly tempting mouth and straight away he felt like loosening his collar because he felt too warm. Memory was pelting him with images he had put away a long time ago. Ava in a little silver shimmery slip of a dress, lithe curves only hinted at, legs that went on for ever. He breathed in slow and deep. The *taste* of Ava's mouth, her hands running up beneath his jacket over his shirt in an incredibly arousing way. Sex personified and prohibited, absolutely not to be touched under any circumstances. And he had broken the rules, he who never broke such rules, who prided himself on his self-control and decency. True, it had only been a kiss but it had been a kiss that should never have happened and the fallout from it had destroyed his family.

Emerging from that disturbing flash of recollection, Vito was tense as a steel rod. He would sack her, of course he would. Having her in the same office when he would not be moving on until the reorganisation was complete was inappropriate. *Utterly inappropriate*, just like his thoughts. He would not keep the young woman who was responsible for his brother's death in one of his businesses. Nobody would expect him to, nobody would condemn his reasoning. But quick as a flash he knew someone who would have done... Olly, caring, compassionate Olly, who had once acted as the voice of Vito's unacknowledged conscience.

Ava moved unsteadily past him, bright head high, refusing to show weakness or concern. Vito was tough, hard, ruthless and brutally successful in a business environment, willing to take a risk and fly in the face of adversity, everything Olly had never been. And yet that had not been the whole story either, Ava conceded painfully, for, macho as Vito undoubtedly was he had been so supportive of the news that Olly was gay, admitting that he had already guessed. Vito had suspected why, like Ava, Olly was the odd one out at school.

And she still remembered Olly laughing and joking in enormous relief at his brother's wholehearted acceptance.

A prickling wash of tears burned below Ava's lowered lids and a flood of anguished grief gripped her for the voice she would never hear again, for the supportive friend she had grown to love.

CHAPTER TWO

THE film of dampness in her eyes only slowly receding, Ava shook her bright head as though to clear it and glanced around herself. The office was massive with an ocean of wooden flooring surrounding a contemporary desk and one corner filled with relaxed seating and a coffee table. Everything was tidy, not one thing out of place, and it exactly depicted Vito's organised, stripped-back style, the desk marred only by a laptop and a single sheaf of documents.

'I couldn't believe it when I recognised you,' Vito admitted flatly.

'It was just as much of a shock for me. I didn't know you owned this business.' Ava's strained eyes darted over him, absorbing the strong angle of his cheekbones, the stubborn jut of his chin and then falling helpless into the melted honey of his beautiful eyes. Eyes the shade of old gold, fringed by outrageously long and luxuriant black lashes. Her heart started to pound as if he had pressed a button somewhere in her body and her mouth ran dry as a bone.

'What are you doing here?' he demanded sardonically. 'I assumed you'd reapply to medical school once you were released.'

Ava froze, her facial muscles tightening. 'No—'

Vito frowned. 'Why not? I'll agree you couldn't expect the university to hold open your place until you got out of prison but you were a brilliant student and I'm sure they would be willing to reconsider you.'

Ava stared steadily back at him but she wasn't really focusing on him any longer. 'That time's gone. I can't go back there…' She hesitated, reluctantly recalling how excited she and Olly had been when they had both received offers to study medicine at the same university. It was unthinkable to her that she could now try to reclaim what Olly had for ever lost because of her. 'I'm here because I needed a job, a way of supporting myself.'

An enquiring ebony brow quirked in surprise. 'Your family?'

Ava raised her chin. 'They don't bother with me now. I haven't heard from any of them since I was sentenced.'

'They are taking a very tough line,' Vito commented, suppressing a stab of pity for her that he felt was inapt.

'They can't forgive me for letting them down.'

'People forgive much worse. You were still a foolish teenager.'

Ava snatched in a shuddering breath, her hands knotting into fists by her sides. 'Have *you* forgiven me?'

Vito went very still, his body rigid with sudden screaming tension, his face hard beneath his bronzed skin. His cloaked eyes lashed back to her with a hint of flaring gold, bright as an eagle hunting for prey. 'I can't.'

Ava felt as sick as if he had punched her and she didn't know how she had dared to ask that crazy question or even why she had asked it. What other answer could she have expected from Olly's brother?

'He was the only family I had,' Vito breathed in curt continuation, his handsome mouth compressing into a harsh line.

Ava was trembling. 'He was pretty much irreplaceable. So what now?' she asked baldly, forcing herself to move away from the topic of Olly before she lost control and embarrassed herself even more. 'You can't want me working here even temporarily.'

'I don't,' Vito admitted grimly, for he had far too many unsettling memories attached to her and his brother and he hated such reminders. He swung away from her with surprising grace for so large a man and moved behind his desk. She *needed* the job, the chance to take up her life again. He recognised that: he just didn't want her doing it around him. She had stolen Olly's life and now she had her own back. Or did she? Her entire family had cut her loose. She had also given up her dream of becoming a doctor. Where was his sense of fair play? Did he usually kick people when they were already down and out? She was struggling: he could see it in the shaky set of that luscious mouth, in the fierce tension of her slim body. Given the opportunity his little brother would, he knew, have urged him not to punish Ava for what had happened. Typical Olly, always the peacemaker, Vito reflected broodingly, his even white teeth gritting as he searched inside himself for some similar strain of compassion and found only the yawning emptiness that the loss of his brother had created.

'So do you want me to leave immediately?' Ava enquired flatly, fighting to keep the unsteadiness out of her voice.

Vito didn't want to look at her because she was making him feel like a bully and, whatever he was, he was not that. He glanced down at his desk and inspiration struck him in the form of the Christmas list lying there. That would be perfect: it would get her out of the office and she revelled in all that Christmas bull so it could not be viewed as a punishment either. From what he could see she had already had her punishment.

'No, you can stay for the moment,' he breathed harshly, thinking that he could shift her elsewhere after the festive season was over and it would cause a lot less comment. 'I have a task I want you to take care of for me...'

Shocked by that sudden turnaround when she had been so sure he was going to sack her, Ava moved quickly forward, too quickly for her ill-fitting shoes. She stepped out of one shoe, having forgotten to clench her toes in it for staying power. 'What is it?'

'What is wrong with your shoes?' Vito demanded impatiently as she lurched to an uneven halt to thrust her foot back into the item.

'They don't fit.'

'Why not?'

Ava reddened. 'Everything I'm wearing is second hand.'

Distaste filled Vito at the mere idea of wearing someone else's clothing.

Recognising his reaction, Ava turned pale with chagrin. 'Look, the last time I was free I was eighteen and wearing Goth clothes. I've grown out of that and I couldn't turn up here to work in a pair of old jeans.'

Vito pulled his wallet out, withdrew a wad of banknotes and extended it to her. 'Buy yourself some shoes,' he told her drily.

Ava was aghast at the gesture. 'I can't take *your* money.'

'You're planning to refuse your salary?'

'No, but that's different,' she argued. 'It's not personal.'

'This isn't personal either. You might try to sue us if you have an accident and you're not much use to anyone round here when you can't walk properly,' Vito fielded without hesitation as he reached for the document, eager to get her back out of his office. 'And you'll probably be doing a lot of walking.'

'What are you talking about?'

He handed her the sheet of paper and the money together. She was close enough to pick up on the spicy scent of his cologne and note the flexing of lean strong muscle below his shirt as he leant forward, compensating for the height difference between them. At over six feet tall, he towered over her five feet four inches. All too readily, however, she remembered the warm, solid feel of his muscular chest below her palms and she stiffened defensively. When he came close, she still wanted to touch him; it was that simple. Guilt assailed her when she thought about the way she had once behaved in his radius.

'It's my Christmas list for the associates we give presents to. Karen Harper will issue you with a company credit card and you will follow the suggestions and go out and gather them all up. OK?' Vito spelt out shortly, his smouldering gaze pinned to the damp pink pout of her mouth.

What was it about her that ensnared him? Vito wondered in frustration, feeling the tight heaviness and drag of response at his groin. While she seemed naively un-

aware of her own sexual power he was all too aware
that he found everything about her, from that peachy
mouth to the tightness of her blouse over her full round
breasts and the fit of her trousers, ridiculously tempting. He wanted her. He wanted to bed her so badly it
almost hurt to think that he could never have her and
the very thought of that shocked him afresh. It had been
so long since a woman affected him on a visceral level.
The last time had been with her, in fact, and that bothered him, bothered him in a way he didn't appreciate
being bothered. No, he definitely didn't want her under
his feet during his working day.

Ava looked up at him in surprise and clashed involuntarily with scorching dark golden eyes of such stormy
beauty she could hardly breathe. A tingling sensation
ran through her, tightening her nipples like a sudden
blast of cold air, although there was nothing chilly about
the well of heat building low in her pelvis.

'You want me to go shopping?' she queried disbe-
lievingly. 'But I'm not a girly girl.'

'Nevertheless if you want to retain employment here
you will do as you are told,' Vito countered drily.

Ava flushed and nibbled at the soft underside of her
lower lip, the tip of her tongue slicking out to ease the
dryness there, while she swallowed back the spark of
temper he had ignited. His innate dominance and self-
assurance had always set her teeth on edge. His way or
the highway, she got that message loud and clear and it
was nothing new to her. She was used to rules now, accustomed to respecting the pecking order to stay safe.
That she should have to do the same thing to stay em-
ployed should not be a surprise.

'Don't do that with your mouth…and don't look at me like that,' Vito chastised.

Look at him in what way? If the look had been inappropriate, she had been unaware of the fact and her chin came up at a mutinous angle. 'I don't know what you're talking about.'

He dealt her an unimpressed scrutiny, dark eyes brilliant and shielded by his lush lashes. 'Don't play the temptress with me. Been there, done that.'

In the state of tension she was in that insolent warning was the tipping point. Lashed by memories of the humiliation he had once inflicted on her, Ava flushed as incandescent rage lit her up like an internal fireworks display. 'Let's get this straight now, Vito,' she bit out furiously. 'I'm no longer that silly infatuated girl you once called a tease! I'm a whole lot wiser than I used to be. You're like a lot of other men—you don't take responsibility for your own behaviour.'

'And what's that supposed to mean?' Vito shot back at her rawly, unprepared for that sudden attack.

'I'm not some fatally seductive Eve, whom no poor male can resist. What happened that night wasn't entirely my fault. You came on to me, you kissed me because you *wanted* to, not because I somehow *made* you do it!' Ava shot back with angry emphasis, blue eyes star-bright with condemnation. 'Deal with your own share of the blame and don't try to foist it on me!'

Wrath blasted through Vito like a cleansing flame, wiping away every other complex reaction that she stirred. That fast he wanted to kill her and it was not the first time she had done that to him. He had dealt with the blame a long time ago but that did not alter the fact that she had used her body around him like a lethal weapon, deliberately stoking the kind of desire that no principled adult wanted to experience in a teenager's radius. It had been a recipe for disaster and had it not been for the car crash that had followed he would have remained satisfied by the outcome of their confrontation. But while he had tried to nip the situation in the bud Ava's fiery temperament had ensured that it had blown up in his face instead.

'I have no intention of discussing the past with you,' Vito delivered crushingly. 'Go buy the shoes and start on the Christmas list, Ava.'

It was a direct order and she was tempted to ignore it when every fibre in her body was still primed for battle. She wanted to defend herself, she had never got the chance to defend herself against his cutting allegations because Olly had interrupted them. But as she had reminded him she was no longer the teenager who had once found it almost impossible to control her emotions. She breathed in slow and deep and, giving him a look that would have daunted a lesser man, she turned round and headed for the door.

'Yes, you have grown up,' Vito remarked silkily, having the last word.

Her teeth clenched, her slender hands curling into tight fists but her spine stayed straight and her mouth firmly closed. Deep down inside she might want to scream at him, shake him...*kiss* him? The shock of that stray thought cooled her temper as nothing else could have done. Although she had got over her crush on him a long time ago, she had also spent the last three years in an all-female environment, forced to repress every sexual instinct, she reasoned impatiently. It was hardly surprising that exposure to a male of Vito's stunning good looks and high-powered sexuality, not to mention the memory of how she had once felt about him, could now make her vulnerable. So, take a chill pill, she urged herself impatiently, you're only human and he's the equivalent of toxic bait to a rat. He might have spectacular packaging but he also had a brain like a computer in which actual emotion had very little input. Even at eighteen she had appreciated that Vito's fondness for his little brother was the sole Achilles' heel in his tough and ruthlessly maintained emotional armour. She had not required Olly's warning to appreciate that she and Vito were chalk and cheese in every way that mattered. Money and success mattered way more to Vito than people. He kept other human beings at a distance and rarely allowed anyone into his inner circle or his private life. She did not count his affairs in that category for, according to what she had witnessed on the sidelines of his life, more sex than feeling was involved in those relationships.

Karen Harper was just replacing the phone when Ava entered her office and she wore an expression like a cat facing a saucer of sour cream. 'Company credit card, right?' she checked icily.

Ava nodded and presented the Christmas list. The brunette gave it a cursory glance. 'You appreciate that I will be checking your purchases very closely,' she spelt out warningly. 'I also advise you to stay strictly within budget. In fact your main objective should be to *save* money rather than spend it.'

'Of course.'

'Obviously Mr Barbieri believes you're up to the challenge because he knows your family,' Karen commented curtly, making her own poor opinion of the decision crystal clear. 'But unfortunately shopping is not work.'

'I just do what I'm told to do,' Ava fielded and turned on her heel, hoping that being at an enjoyable distance from Karen for a couple of days would ultimately do her no harm.

Ava returned to her allotted desk to go over the list and make plans. Saving money? When it came to the question of saving money she was, without a doubt, the go-to girl for she had never had enough cash to get by comfortably. Even though her family had always lived well, Ava had rarely been given money and had survived during term time at school through a series of part-time holiday jobs waiting tables and stacking shelves. Studying the list, she dug out Marge's catalogue to see if any suitable substitutes could be found within those pages. Surely charitable gifts would be more acceptable during a period of economic austerity when most people were feeling the pinch? She did a little homework on the computer to find out what she could about the interests of the recipients and hit pay dirt several times on that score, making helpful notes beside those names. That achieved, she paused only to pin a picture of Harvey to the office noticeboard in the forlorn hope that the dog might take someone's fancy. Marge had said Harvey could stay only two more weeks in her home as she was expecting the usual influx of abandoned and surrendered animals that followed the festive season. Ava tried to picture Harvey with a bow in his hair as a much-wanted gift and frowned: he just wasn't cute and fluffy enough to attract that kind of owner. But he was such a *loving* animal, Ava reflected painfully, knowing that the dog would have to be put to sleep at the vets' surgery if she could not find him a home. How could she have been so irresponsible as to let herself get attached to him?

When she left AeroCarlton, Ava went straight to buy a pair of shoes because the muscles in her feet were aching at the effort it took to keep the second-hand ones on. As soon as she could she would pay Vito back. Although she then made a start on the Christmas list unfortunate images continued to bombard her brain at awkward moments, scattering her thoughts and disturbing her. She didn't want to think about the night of the party but suddenly she couldn't think of anything else.

Every year Vito held a Christmas party for his senior staff, estate employees, tenants and neighbours. It was the equivalent of the local squire of Victorian times throwing open his grand doors to the public. That last year Ava had become so obsessed by Vito that she wouldn't even go out on a date with anyone else.

'It's unhealthy to be so intense,' Olly had told her in frustration that winter. 'You can't have Vito. He's not into teenagers and never will be. In his eyes you're only one step removed from a child.'

'I'll be nineteen in April and I'm mature for my age,' she had protested.

'Says who?' Olly had parried unimpressed, his blond blue-eyed and open face as far removed from his half-brother's as day is to night for he had inherited his English mother's looks rather than his Italian father's. 'A mature woman would never have got that tattoo on her hip!'

And, of course, Olly had been correct on that score, Ava acknowledged ruefully. An alcohol-induced decision on a sixth form holiday abroad had resulted in that piece of nonsense. She had marked herself for life over a teenage infatuation and needed no-one to tell her how foolish that was. When she eventually worked up the courage to get naked with a guy she knew she would cringe if there was any need to make an explanation.

In the present her mind careened back to that disastrous party when, for a change, she had gone all out to look sophisticated and had abandoned her Goth attire for the evening. Not that she wasn't fully aware at the time that her regular appearances in short black leather skirts and boots attracted Vito's attention! Did that make her a tease? She had seen girls out on the town wearing much more provocative clothing. Admittedly Vito's frighteningly elegant girlfriends had never appeared in such apparel. But just for once at the Christmas party Vito had been single with no eager possessive beauty clinging to his arm like a limpet and laughing and smiling at his every word.

From the first moment when Ava had met Vito Barbieri when she was sixteen there had been a buzz when their eyes met. It had taken her more than a year to reach the conclusion that he felt that buzz too but that he was fighting it tooth and nail. He had never said a word out of place and had been careful to stay out of reach and treat her more than ever like a little girl. But more than once she had been conscious of his eyes on her and the burn of satisfaction that minor triumph had given her had merely encouraged her to visit the castle when Vito was in residence. That he could be attracted to her and *never* do anything about it had not once crossed her mind as a possibility. It didn't matter how often Olly warned her that she was wasting her time dreaming about Vito. As long as Ava was aware that

the attraction was mutual she had cherished the hope
that eventually he would succumb.

With hindsight that insouciant confidence of hers
made Ava recoil in mortification. How could she ever
have truly believed that Vito might date her? The daughter of one of his employees, whose father lived with his
family near Bolderwood Castle? His little brother's best
friend? An eighteen-year-old still at school studying
for her final exams with no experience and no decent
clothes? Unfortunately, the depth of her obsession with
him had ensured she ignored all common sense when
he was around.

Her whole family had attended that party. Ava had
worn a silver shift dress, cut down from a maxi that her
sister, Gina, had put out for recycling. Somehow there
had never been money to buy new clothes for Ava. The
dress had been simple, even modest, and she had been
careful with her make-up and her hair, keen neither to
shock nor repel. She had seen Vito watching her from
the doorway while she was dancing with the children
she was helping to look after at their separate party in
another room. Needing to stoke her confidence, she had
been drinking, something she was usually more careful *not* to do, always fearful that her mother's weakness
might some day turn out to be hers as well.

Ava no longer remembered when she had first appreciated that her mother was different from other moth-
ers. She had often come home from primary school and
found her mother out for the count on her bed. But then
Ava's had never been a happy home because her parents fought like cat and dog. Furthermore, her mother
had always been distant with her. And with a father
who called her 'Ginger' if he called her anything, even

though he knew how much it hurt her feelings to suffer
that hated nickname in her own home, she had never
suffered from the illusion that she was a much-wanted
child. A full ten years younger than her eldest sister,
Bella, Ava had often wondered if she was an unplanned
accident resented by both her parents for neither of them
had ever had any time for her.

But for all that she had loved her mother, Gemma
Fitzgerald's death while Ava was in prison had been
a severe shock and source of grief for she had long
hoped that as she got older she might finally forge a
closer relationship with her parent. In her teens she had
realised that her mother had a serious problem with
alcohol and was sober only in the morning, getting pro-
gressively drunker throughout the day on her hidden
stashes of booze round the house until she was usually
slumped comatose on the sofa by early evening. Ava's
father and sisters had studiously ignored Gemma's al-
coholism and done everything they could to cover it
up. Divorce had been mentioned but never rehabilitation until the night her mother was caught driving while
under the influence by the police and her father's puni-
tive rage had known no bounds when the incident was
reported in the local paper. Gemma had lost her licence
and gone into rehab, returning home from the experience pale, quiet and mercifully sober.

Having noticed Vito watching her the night of the
Christmas party, Ava had decided to take the bull by the
horns, a decision that she would live to regret. She had
tracked Vito down to the quiet of the library where he
was standing by the fire with a drink in his hand. Tall,
darkly beautiful and powerful, he had riveted her from
the minute she walked through the door.

'What do you want?' he had demanded edgily.

Ava had perched on the side of the desk in a way that best displayed her long shapely legs and put her directly in front of him. As she had carefully adjusted the hem to a decent length she had felt his eyes on her as hot as the flames in the fire and excitement had filled her like a dangerous drug urging her on. 'I want you,' she told him boldly, no longer content to only offer lingering looks and encouraging smiles in invitation.

Vito treated her to a brooding look of derision that dented her pride right where it hurt most. 'You couldn't handle me,' he countered drily. 'Go and find some boy your own age to practise your wiles on.'

'You want me too,' Ava responded doggedly for, having started, she found it quite impossible to retreat with dignity and she stabbed on regardless with her sui-cidal mission to make him finally acknowledge what she believed already lay between them. 'Did you think I wouldn't notice?'

'It's time you went home and sobered up,' Vito re-torted with scorn. 'This conversation is likely to em-barrass you tomorrow.'

Ava continued to stare at him with unconcealed long-ing, her blue eyes languorous, her soft pink mouth pout-ing in reproach at his refusal to match her honesty. 'I don't embarrass that easily and I am well over the age of consent.'

'Your body might be but your brain is way behind,' Vito riposted, shifting closer in a fluid step that made her heart race. 'Go home, Ava. I don't want this non-sense.'

'I would be much more fun than any of those women

I've seen you bring back here!' she challenged. 'I'm not the clingy type.'

Vito stopped dead right in front of her. 'I'm not looking for fun. You've got nothing I want…and a little word of warning. Most men prefer to do their own chasing. Your in-my-face approach is a complete turn-off.'

Colour flamed into Ava's cheeks at his blunt rejection of what she had to offer. She snaked off the desktop in a surge of temper and wrapped her arms round his neck to prevent him from backing away from her. 'I do not turn you off,' she argued vehemently, gazing up into his dark golden eyes, which were spectacular in the firelight. 'That's a total lie! Why won't you tell the truth for once?'

'Ava…' Vito groaned in frustration, reaching up to detach her hands from his neck.

But before he could do so she stretched up and kissed him with every atom of craving she possessed. The muscles in his lean, strong body turned rigid and then he suddenly crushed her lips under his, his tongue spearing hungrily down into the tender interior of her mouth to make her literally shudder with excitement and a blissful sense of coming home. That single kiss was like dynamite to her self-control. With an eager gasp of response she melted into him, bones turning to mush under the onslaught of the piercing hunger gathering low in her pelvis. A door opened but she didn't hear it, reacting only when it slammed shut again.

'Vito…for heaven's sake, what are you doing?' Olly yelled in dismay. 'Let her go!'

Vito thrust Ava away roughly from him, the distaste on his face unmistakable. 'You're a calculating little tease…and you won't take no for an answer.'

'I'm not a t—'

Olly closed his hand round her forearm. 'Time to go home, Ava. I'll drive you.'

Ava's head swivelled, her furious eyes pinned to Vito's shuttered face in condemnation. 'How dare you call me a tease?' she launched at him as a sense of humiliation engulfed her, for she had made her last desperate move and he was still rebuffing her, resolutely refusing to acknowledge the sense of connection between them.

For the very first time in the immediate aftermath of that encounter Ava worried that her feelings were entirely one-sided. Was it possible that a man could be attracted to a woman without actually wanting to act on it? The same way people could admire a painting in a museum without needing to own it? That humiliating realisation came crashing down on Ava like a big black storm cloud. Her last recollection of that evening was of rushing down the steps of the castle in floods of tears with Olly chasing after her, urging her to calm down. The image that came next in her memory was waking up in hospital with a mind that was a terrifying blank, the events of the previous evening only returning slowly over the following days in jagged bits and pieces. But she had never been able to fully recall that car journey or the crash. Her defence had made much of the yawning gaps in her memory during her trial.

But ignorance had not protected her even from her own painful questions. How could she have got behind a steering wheel in the state she had been in? She had never been able to answer that question to her own satisfaction. Even more saliently, the car had belonged to Olly and he had been sober so why on earth had he allowed her to drive when she wasn't insured to drive his car?

Shoulders bowing beneath the stress of recalling her stupid selfishness that evening, Ava focused her swimming eyes on the Christmas list and resolved to get on with the task at hand. Revisiting the past, she decided, was a very bad idea when her mistakes had resulted in indefensible behaviour and tragic consequences.

CHAPTER THREE

'COMPLETE junk!' Karen Harper pronounced triumphantly, laying a cushion woven with an image of a dog down on Vito's desk. 'Ava has made a complete pig's ear of the Christmas list and bought ridiculous gifts! She'll have to return the stuff and someone else will have to take charge of the list.'

An expression of exasperation crossed Vito's face for he did not appreciate having his busy morning interrupted by inconsequential dramas. He had only given Ava the list to get her out of the office and was in no mood for fallout from that decision. He swept up the phone. 'Ask Ava Fitzgerald to join us,' he told his PA.

Ava was sheltering in the cloakroom, cheeks still burning after a mortifyingly public scene with the dissatisfied office manager. Having done what she had been asked to the best of her ability, Ava had been furious when Karen Harper looked over her carefully chosen purchases and labelled her 'an idiot' in front of her co-workers. She accepted that she was just a junior but felt that even a junior employee deserved a certain modicum of respect and consideration. Her pale heart-shaped face tight, she finished renewing her lip gloss and moved away from the mirror.

'Mr Barbieri wants to speak to you,' Vito's PA, a glamorous blonde in her early thirties, informed Ava in the corridor.

Ava walked stoically back into Vito's office. Twenty-four hours had passed since their last encounter and after the restless night she had suffered while she fretted over what could not be changed she wished it had been longer. Getting out of bed to face another day had been a challenge. Having to deal with a man who despised her was salt in an already open wound. That he was the same guy she had once loved hammered her pride to smithereens.

Vito, a devastatingly elegant figure in a charcoal grey suit expertly tailored to his tall, powerful physique, viewed her with cool precision, the sooty lashes that ringed his remarkable eyes visible even at a distance. He indicated the cushion. 'Ava…care to explain this?'

'Matt Aiken and his wife breed Labradors and show them at Crufts. I thought the cushions were the perfect gift.'

'What about that ugly pottery vase?' Karen Harper broke in.

'Made by a charity in Mumbai that supports homeless widows,' Ava explained. 'Ruhina Dutta is very forthright about the needs of minorities in India. I thought she would appreciate the vase and a charitable donation more than she would appreciate perfume,' Ava continued levelly, encountering an unreadable look from Vito that made her even tenser. She could not tell whether he approved of her outlook or not, but that lingering scrutiny sent high-wire energy shooting through her like lightning rods.

'And that silly chain from Tiffany's?' Karen was in

no mood to back down. 'It doesn't even have a proper catch—'

'Because it's a spectacles chain. Mrs Fox complained in a recent interview that she is always mislaying her glasses.'

Vito released a short laugh, his impatience with the subject unconcealed. Ava went pink, noting that he was now avoiding looking directly at her and feeling ignored even though she told herself that it was stupid to feel that way. Surely she no longer wanted his attention?And if he wanted to treat her like the office junior she was supposed to be, she would have to get used to receiving as much attention as the paint on the wall.

'What about all that animal-orientated stuff you've bought?' Karen demanded sharply. 'It's unacceptable for you to only buy gifts from your favourite charity.'

'A lot of people on that list have pets. You told me to save money if I could.'

'I certainly didn't tell you to buy junk!' Karen Harper snapped.

'Some of the proposed gifts on the list were incredibly expensive and at a time when so many people are cutting back, those suggestions struck me as OTT,' Ava admitted in a rueful undertone. 'But, of course, anything I've bought can be changed if required.'

'That won't be necessary. Finish the job—you've obviously done your homework on the recipients,' Vito conceded, his strong jaw line squaring as he skimmed a detached glance at Ava and extended the cushion to her. 'But I don't like to waste my time on trivia. Please remove this difference of opinion from my office.'

The office manager stiffened. 'Of course, Mr Barbieri. I'm sorry I interrupted you.'

The other woman insisted on checking the remainder of the list with Ava before she went out shopping again. Ava was embarrassed when a couple of co-workers chose that same moment to return Marge's catalogue with orders and cash attached.

'You're here to work, not to sell stuff for your pet charity,' Karen said icily. 'When you get back this afternoon I have several jobs for you to take care of, so be as quick as you can.'

When Ava returned, footsore and laden with carrier bags, Karen took her straight down to the filing cabinets in the basement and gave her enough work to keep her busy into at least the middle of the following week. Ava knew it was a punishment for stepping out of line and accepted it as such without resentment. True the basement was lonely, dull and filled with artificial light but it was a relief to know that she need no longer fear running into Vito. Earlier he had behaved unnervingly like a stranger and she didn't know why that should have surprised her or left her feeling ridiculously resentful. After all, he was the last man in the world from whom she could expect special treatment.

A week later, Vito was studying his companion over lunch in a famous restaurant. By any standards Laura was beautiful with her long blonde fall of hair and almond-shaped brown eyes. She didn't ring his bells though: he thought her mouth was too thin, her voice too sharp and she was painfully fond of bitching about the models she worked with. Was he simply bored? There had to be some reason why his mind constantly wandered, why it had suddenly become a challenge for him to sit still even long enough to eat a meal. The unease that had been nibbling bites out of his self-discipline for days returned in full force.

His day had had an unfortunate start with a call from his estate manager, Damien Keel. Damien, keen to get his festive calendar organised, had asked him if there would be a Christmas party this year at the castle. Ironically it was the first time that Vito had been asked that question since his brother's death but Damien, a relatively new employee, had never been part of that loop. The first year, nobody had asked or expected a party and since then Vito had just quietly ignored that custom. Now, suddenly, he felt guilty about that break with tradition. His staff deserved the treat. Three years was long enough to make a public display of grief. He decided there and then that it was past time he reinstated normality. He glanced at Laura, happily engaged in a very long drawn-out story about yet another rival in the modelling world, and he suppressed his growing impatience. He knew he would be moving on from Laura as well.

Striding back into AeroCarlton, he glanced at Reception. There was no sign of Ava in the general office either. For a gopher she was keeping an exceptionally low profile. It was not that he *wanted* to see her, more that he was steeling himself to accept her presence. But it was a week since he had last laid eyes on her and he was getting curious.

'Is Ava Fitzgerald still working here?' he asked his PA.

'I don't know, sir...'

'Find out,' he instructed.

Ava was in the basement, the layout of which she now knew like the back of her hand. She had filed away

entire boxes of documents, and when she had completed that task Karen had introduced her to her shiny
new and fiendishly complex filing system and put her
to work on it. In the distance she heard the lift clang-
ing as the doors opened and she did not have long to
wait for her visitor.

'Since you won't go out to lunch, I've brought lunch
to you,' a familiar voice announced.

Suppressing a groan, Ava spun round from the cabinet of files she was reorganising and smoothed down
her skirt in a movement that came as naturally as
breathing to her in Pete Langford's radius. Of medium
height and lanky build, Pete looked over her slender
figure in a way that made her feel vaguely unclean. It
was a few days since he had made his first call down
to the basement to chat to her and even her display of
indifference had failed to daunt him. Now he extended
a panini and a soft drink to her while he lounged back
against the bare table in the centre of the room.

'Take a break,' he urged, setting the items down on
the table.

'You shouldn't have bought those.' Her stomach
growled because her tiny budget didn't run to lunches.
'Give them to someone else—I have some shopping
to do.'

'Do it after work. I'm here now,' he pointed out as
if she ought to drop everything to give him some attention.

Ava hated being railroaded and valued her freedom
of choice. She didn't fancy an impromptu lunch with
Pete in the solitude of the basement and had no desire
to drift into a situation where she would have to fight
him off. He was the sort of guy who thought he was

God's gift and who believed persistence would pay off. One of her co-workers had already warned her that he went after all the new girls. 'I'm going to take a break upstairs,' she told him.

Pete sighed. 'What's your problem?'

'I don't have one. I'm just not interested,' Ava told him baldly.

'Are you gay?' Pete demanded abruptly. 'I mean, all that time in prison, I suppose you didn't have much choice...'

Ava lost colour and stiffened. 'Who told you I was in prison?'

'Was it meant to be hush-hush? Everybody knows.'

'It's not something I talk about,' Ava retorted curtly, trying not to react to the news that her past was an open secret amongst her co-workers, some of whom had proved quite reluctant to speak to her. The bite of humiliation, the pain of being the oddity and distrusted while people speculated about her crime, cut deep.

'Who told *you?*' another, harsher male voice enquired from the doorway. 'That was supposed to be confidential information.'

Ava levelled her stunned gaze on Vito. He must have used the stairs because she hadn't heard the lift. He stood at the door, his gorgeous eyes a brilliant scorching gold, his lean strong face hard as granite as he awaited Pete Langford's response. Having heard that last crack about Ava being gay, Vito was taut with outrage and simmering fury. He did not understand why he was so furious to find Ava with another man until it occurred to him that after her prison sentence she was probably a sitting duck for such an approach and that as her employer it surely behoved him to ensure that nobody took advantage of her vulnerability. Not that at that precise moment Ava actually looked vulnerable, he conceded abstractedly. Her eyes were sparkling with angry resentment and her slim but undeniably curvy figure was beautifully sculpted in the black pencil skirt and tight-fitting red shirt she wore. Without any warning, another image was superimposed over her: Ava, amazingly elfin cute in a lace corset top, short black leather skirt and clunky boots. Startled, he blinked, but the damage had been done and he was left willing back a surge of arousal.

Pete Langford had turned shaken eyes onto his employer. 'I don't remember who first mentioned Ava's background,' he mumbled evasively, his former attitude of relaxation evaporating fast below Vito's intimidating stare. 'Look, I'd better get back upstairs.'

'What a good idea,' Vito pronounced deadpan, his big powerful body taut with silent menace.

As the lift doors closed on Pete's hurried departure Ava frowned uncertainly. 'What was that all about?'

'How long have you been working down here?' Vito demanded, ignoring the question.

'Since I finished the Christmas list that day I was in your office,' Ava admitted.

'You've been working down here a full week? *Every* day, *all* day?'

In silence, Ava nodded, entrapped by the aura of vibrant energy he emanated. Her gaze locked to his face, scanning the sinful cheekbones, the bold nose and sensual mouth. Suddenly she didn't blame herself any more for having a crush on him at the age of sixteen. After all, he turned female heads wherever he went.

'It must feel like you're back in a cell!' Vito ground

out grimly, scanning the bare comfortless lines of the big room with angry dissatisfaction.

'It's work and I'm grateful to have a job,' Ava countered quietly. 'And if you think this place reminds me of prison, you have no concept of what prison life is like.'

'Putting you down here was not my idea,' Vito informed her grimly.

'I didn't think it was. You're not petty but you did want me out from under your feet and I am literally fulfilling that function here,' she pointed out, dimples appearing as she shot him an irreverent grin.

And that grin lit up her heart-shaped face like the dawn light. She was beautiful. Why had he never realised that before? The fine-boned fragility of her features allied with that transparent complexion and the contrast of that fiery hair was stunning. He didn't like red hair, he reminded himself, at least he had never had a redhead in his bed. Not that he wanted her there either, he told himself fiercely, fighting the heat and tension at his groin to the last ditch of denial. He didn't want her, he had never wanted her, he had just kissed her once because she gave him no other choice. Or was that the excuse she had labelled it? He studied that ripe pink mouth, bare as it was of lipstick, and remembered the taste of her, heady, sweet and unbearably sexy...

Ava's bright blue eyes had widened and darkened. The sparks in the atmosphere were whirling round her faster and faster. It was like standing in the eye of a storm. She moved forward, unconsciously reacting to a sexual tension she could not withstand. Her clothes felt shrink-wrapped to her skin and she was insanely conscious of the swell of her breasts and the tingling tightness of her nipples while the heat between her thighs made her press those offending limbs tightly together.

In the humming silence, Vito stared back. It was all right to look now, he reminded himself sardonically. She was no longer jailbait. The thought cut a chain somewhere inside him, slicing him free of the past. He coiled a hand round her wrist and pulled her into his arms, dark golden eyes volatile, ferocious energy leaping through him in a wild surge of lust.

His other hand lifted slowly and his forefinger traced the fullness of her lower lip, his touch light as a butterfly's wings. Ava almost bit his finger in frustration, her breath escaping her in an audible gasp. Kiss me, kiss me, *kiss me*, she willed him. Her craving was so great at that moment that there was no room for any other thought. He lowered his handsome dark head and drove her lips apart with a passionate kiss, driven by all the hunger pent up in his powerful body. And it was just what she wanted, what thrilled her most, desire leaping through her slight body like a blinding light as his tongue delved into the sensitive interior of her mouth and the world spun in ever faster circles round her. Her knees wobbled and she kissed him back with the same passion, her tongue twinning with his, her breasts crushed to the wall of his hard muscular torso, all awareness centred on sensation and satisfaction. He eased her back from him, long fingers skating up over her taut ribcage to close round one breast, teasing the prominent peak with an expertise that drew a moan from her throat. He set her back from him, took a slow step away, smouldering eyes locked to her like precision lasers.

'This is not the place, *belleza mia*.'

Ava snatched in a gigantic gulp of oxygen to regain control of her treacherous body and the searing disappointment of his withdrawal. But she knew it had cost him, had felt him hard and ready and awesomely male against her, and the awareness soothed her tumultuous emotions as nothing else could have done. *This* time she was not the only one in the grip of that savage wanting.

'I will have you moved from the basement immediately,' Vito told her flatly, not a bit of expression in his deep drawl, his shrewd gaze veiled and closed to her.

'That's not necessary,' Ava declared.

'It is. I hope I deal fairly with all my employees and isolating you in the basement with only boring repetitive work to carry out is not acceptable.'

A little devil danced in her eyes. 'Do you kiss them as well?'

Vito stilled at the door, strong jaw line squaring. 'You're the first,' he confessed darkly.

'Aren't you about to tell me that it won't ever happen again?' Ava prompted, heart in her mouth at the thought.

Vito dealt her a thunderous glance and she went pink, registering in some surprise that she had been teasing him, set on provocation. He headed back to the stairs, still buzzing with aftershocks and the agony of sexual restraint. She could set him on fire with one look, one kiss. He could have quite happily lifted her onto the table, spread those long slim thighs and satisfied them both, but Vito was always distrustful of the new and enticing and preferred to hold back and stay in control. If he could stay in control, he was willing to admit that he wanted Ava Fitzgerald. In fact he wanted her a whole lot more than he had wanted a woman in a long time. Perhaps it was because she had once been forbidden fruit. He examined that possibility but the how and the why couldn't hold his attention. He was free, she was free and she was an adult now. As long as he kept those realities in mind there was nothing more complex at play.

She killed Olly.

Vito stamped on that unwelcome thought and buried it deep. Sex was straightforward. Sex he could handle. He didn't need to think about it or question the authenticity of a basic human urge to mate. She was beautiful and she excited him. And that excitement was rare enough in his life to wipe out every other consideration and finer feeling and take precedence. Of recent, life had been desperately dull apart from the occasional energising business deal. It was the season of goodwill and suddenly he was willing to flow with it.

An hour later, Karen Harper called Ava upstairs to cover the reception desk. She then made coffee for a meeting, tidied the stationery cupboard and ran various errands. The end of the day came much faster than usual and she went straight to Marge's house to collect Harvey for the evening. Marge, delighted at the orders the catalogue had received from various AeroCarlton employees, gave her an evening meal. Afterwards, Ava took Harvey for a long walk and sat on a bench for a while, patting the curly head resting against her thigh and talking to him. Sometimes she could still hardly believe that she was once again living a life that was no longer controlled by strict regulations and ringing bells. Having spent hour after hour locked in a cell, she appreciated the freedom of physical activity. In prison the only exercise she'd had was pacing doggedly round the exercise yard. The open prison, of course, had not been as restrictive and there she had had access to a gym.

When her mobile phone rang she did not initially realise that it was hers and finally wrenched it out of her pocket, believing that it had to be one of her family as she answered it.

'It's Vito. I need your address. I want to speak to you.'

Surprise gripped Ava. She was already on her feet. She reluctantly gave her address, telling herself that it was foolish to be embarrassed about her humble accommodation. He would scarcely expect to find her inhabiting a penthouse apartment. As there wasn't time to return Harvey to Marge's and get back in time to meet Vito, she walked the dog back fast with her. Her mind was working even more actively than her feet.

Vito would want to tell her that the kiss had meant nothing. As if she didn't know that! As if she hadn't got old enough and wise enough yet to appreciate that workaholic billionaires of his calibre didn't come on to the office junior, particularly not when she was a former offender, guilty of causing a tragic car crash that had cost his closest relative his life. Vito, she assumed, had succumbed to a lusty impulse as she had heard even the best of men did occasionally. Was that her fault? she asked herself anxiously. Had her shockingly physical awareness of Vito Barbieri somehow put out the vibes that had lured him into that kiss? It was a lowering suspicion and her chin came up. He had better not try to tell her that she had tempted him again!

CHAPTER FOUR

A SLEEK silver limo with a driver was parked outside the building where Ava lived. As she hurried down the street lined with weathered and grimy brick-fronted houses Vito emerged from the back seat, looking every bit as immaculate in his dark cashmere overcoat and suit as he had earlier. Her hair was wind-tousled, her make-up long since worn off, and her shabby jeans and fleece jacket far from flattering but she told herself that she didn't care. How could you even begin to impress a guy who had everything and dated international models and celebrities?

'Ava...'

'This is Harvey. Be nice,' Ava urged as Harvey growled. 'Show me your paw.'

Somewhat taken aback, Vito watched the hairy dog sit and raise a paw, round doggy eyes pinned to him with suspicion. 'You have a pet?'

'No, actually. Harvey's a stray who needs a home. I'm not allowed to keep a dog here. I live on the third floor.'

'This isn't a good area for a woman living alone,' Vito remarked following her up the stairs.

'Did you think I hadn't noticed?' Ava asked, unlocking her door and stepping inside before bending down to free Harvey from his lead.

Disconcerted by that mocking reply, Vito watched the worn denim flex over her curvy derrière. The more he saw of the sleek elegant lines of her body, the more he liked it. His fingers curled into loose fists. 'I don't like to think of you living round here...although at least you have a watchdog.'

'I can't keep Harvey here overnight. I'll have to take him back to Marge's later.'

'Who's Marge?'

'She runs a small boarding kennels and takes in strays. I worked there for a few months while I was in an open prison. I still help out when I can. She has a whole network of volunteers, who provide foster homes for strays and try to rehome them. The same people also make those dog cushions and the like to sell for funds,' she explained.

Vito had already lost interest. As Harvey settled on the rug by the single bed Vito paced deeper into the small room to take a considering look at the shabby furniture and the severe lack of personal effects and comforts. The rug on the linoleum floor was the sole luxury. 'I can't believe your family are leaving you to live like this.'

'Look, living here is a lot more comfortable and private than a hostel dormitory would be,' Ava replied with spirit. 'Would you like coffee?'

'I've just had a meal. I'm fine,' Vito responded with a polite nod, stationing himself by the dirty window. He noticed that his breath was misting in the air; there was no heating. He was appalled to find her living in such surroundings and no longer marvelled at the fact that she had been wearing second-hand shoes.

'You can take your coat off—I promise not to steal it!'

'It's too cold in here.'

Ava crouched down to switch on the gas fire. She used it for an hour every evening to heat the room before she went to bed. She smiled to herself. Vito might be tough but he loved heat. If there was no sunlight he had to have a fire on. Olly used to tease him about it. At the thought her smile died away as quickly as it had come and she wondered if she would ever be in Vito's company without remembering the awful loss she had inflicted on him.

'You said you wanted to speak to me,' she reminded him, turning to face him.

His eyes glittered like black diamonds in the light from the lamp by the bed. 'I have a suggestion to put to you.'

Ava rested her head to one side, copper-red hair glinting like fire across her dark jacket, strands of honey gold lightening the overall effect.

'You look like a robin when you do that.'

Ava didn't want to be compared to a bird. Since when was a robin stylish or sexy? It was more of a perky, cheeky bird, she reasoned, and then flushed at the way her mind was working, seeking a compliment, approval, anything other than his indifference, that was her and it was pathetic at her age to still be so needy!

'I want to hold the Christmas party again this year,' Vito continued doggedly. 'Well, I don't really *want* to but I believe it's time.'

'You mean you haven't had one…*since*?' Ava completed, her voice cracking a little on that final emphatic word, which encompassed so much.

A haunted darkness filled Vito's stunning eyes, revealing a clear glimpse of pain, and it tore up something inside her. 'No, not for three years,' he responded flatly.

'OK…' Recognising that further enquiry would be unwelcome, Ava strove to match his detached attitude and ram down the pained feelings swelling inside her that sometimes felt too big and powerful to hold in. 'So?' she prompted jerkily, wondering what the subject could possibly have to do with her.

'I want you to organise it—the party, the decoration of the house, the whole festive parade,' Vito extended, a sardonic look on his handsome face.

'*Me?* You want *me* to organise it?' Ava was incredulous at the idea, utterly filled with disbelief.

'You and Olly always took care of it for me before,' Vito reminded her, noting how very white she had become, the subject no easier for her than it was for him. 'I want you to do it again, deal with the caterers and all the fuss. I won't be involved but I think my staff and neighbours should feel free to enjoy the event again.'

Finally, Ava accepted that he was making a genuine request but it did not remove her astonishment. 'You can't have thought this through. Me? Have you any idea what people would think and say about me doing the arrangements for the party again?'

Vito raised an incredulous brow. 'I have never in my life stopped to worry about what other people think,' he countered with resounding assurance. 'It strikes me as the perfect solution. You will recreate Christmas in the same spirit as Olly did. The two of you revelled in all that traditional nonsense.'

Ava dragged in a ragged breath and had to literally swallow down the unnecessary reminder that Olly was gone. Nonsense, yes, she recalled helplessly, Vito had always believed the seasonal festivities were nonsense, only excepting those of a religious persuasion from his censure. Even so, he had tolerated her and Olly's efforts to capture the magic of Christmas with the same long-suffering indulgence that an adult awarded childish passions.

'I suggest you stay at AeroCarlton for what remains of the week and move into the castle at the weekend.'

'M-move into the castle?' Ava stammered, shaken at the suggestion.

'You can hardly do the work from here,' Vito pointed out, his measured drawl as cool as ice on her skin.

Christmas at Bolderwood, the stuff of dreams, Ava conceded abstractedly and familiar images washed through her mind: gathering holly and ivy from the forest, choosing the tree and dressing it, eating mince pies by the fire in the Great Hall. Even as she felt sick with longing at the recollection of happier times something snapped shut as tight as a padlock inside her brain. Christmas *without* Olly in what had once been Olly's happy home: it was unthinkable. She didn't deserve it, couldn't even consider such an undertaking when she had for ever destroyed Christmas for Vito.

'I couldn't do it. It would be a frightful mistake to use me. It would offend people.'

'If it does not offend me, why should it offend anyone else?' Vito enquired with arrogant conviction. 'You're over-sensitive, Ava. You can't live in the past for ever.'

'You can't forgive me!' Ava suddenly cried in jagged protest. 'How do you expect me to forgive myself?'

Vito cursed her emotional turbulence. Everything he controlled she expressed, but he saw her attitude as another sign that he was taking the right path. 'It's three years. It might feel like it only happened yesterday but it's been three years,' he pointed out harshly. 'Life has to go on. Make this Christmas a proper tribute to Olly's memory.'

Ava was struggling to suppress such a giant surge of emotion that her legs trembled under her and she braced her hand on the back of a chair, her eyes stinging with a rush of tears. Olly's memory. It always hurt too much to examine her memories of him and then be forced to accept the reality of his death again.

'Do you really think that my brother would have wanted to see you living like this?' Face taut, eyes ablaze with impatience, Vito lifted both arms in an unusually dramatic gesture of derision.

Ava's chin came up at that question and her spine straightened. 'No, I know he wouldn't have wanted this,' she admitted grudgingly, blinking back the tears that had almost shamed her. 'But I can't help it.'

'*Che cosa hai!* What's the matter with you?' Vito reproved, his dark deep voice growling over the vowel sounds. 'You're a fighter—I expected more from you.'

Mortified colour sprang up over her cheekbones, flooding her porcelain pale skin like the dawn on his Tuscan estate. That stray thought, far too colourful for a man who considered himself imaginative only in business, set his even white teeth on edge. He looked at her, grimly appraising her appearance in shabby clothes. Hair like molten copper in an unflattering ponytail, face dominated by bright blue eyes and that luscious mouth, garments too shapeless and poorly fitting to compliment

even her slender figure. Nothing there to fascinate or tit-
illate, he reasoned impatiently, but his attention roamed
back to her delicate features and lingered. A split second later he was hard as a rock, his blood drumming
through the most sensitive part of his body as he imagined that succulent mouth pleasuring him.

'Yes, I'm a fighter,' Ava breathed shakily, gazing
back at him, feeling the change in the atmosphere and
finding it quite impossible to ignore it. How could he
make her feel this way without even trying? All right,
he was very good-looking but surely she should have
outgrown her teenaged sensitivity to his attraction? The
pulse low in her pelvis was a nagging ache and she spun
away restively, determined to get a grip on her physical
reactions. After all, he had just challenged her pride,
her belief in herself, and she could not let that stand unanswered. She might be afraid of other people's reactions to her, but she was not prepared to admit the fact
that rejection still hurt her way more than it should have
done. 'If you really want me to, I'll do it…Christmas for
you but don't blame me if people think you're crazy.'

Vito had fixed his brilliant eyes to Harvey, who had
practically merged with the hearth rug in his relaxation.
'I've already told you how much I care about that.'

'Yes, but—'

'I prefer women who agree with me.'

'No, you do not!' Ava snapped back. 'You just get
bored and walk all over them!'

Vito felt that even walking over her might be fun
and his black lashes dropped low on his reflective eyes.
He was still in an odd mood, he acknowledged in exasperation, a mood of unease where random thoughts
clouded his usually crystal-clear brain. He wondered if it

was the season or talking about Olly that had disturbed him and settled for that obvious explanation with relief. 'Staying at the castle may give you the opportunity to see your family again.'

'It will shock them, annoy them, as they've made it quite clear they don't want me back in their lives,' she pointed out heavily. 'But that's their right and I have to accept it.'

Vito made no comment, still taken aback by what he had done. A spur of the moment idea had fired him up with an almost missionary zeal to make changes. Putting Ava in charge of Christmas was as much for her benefit as his own. It would toughen him up, banish the atrocious vulnerability that afflicted and destabilised him whenever he thought about his little brother. That was a weakness that Vito could not accept and he could no longer live with it and the necessity of constantly suppressing negative responses. He thought of all the people who had recommended therapy to deal with his grief and his beautifully moulded mouth took on a derisive slant. Therapy wasn't his style. He didn't discuss such things with strangers, nor would he ever have sought professional help for a loss he deemed to be a perfectly normal, if traumatic, life experience. He was *totally* capable of dealing with his own problem and by the end of the Christmas party, when Ava Fitzgerald departed from his life again, he would have finally made an important step in the recovery process. Avoiding her, acting all touchy-feely sensitive as he saw it, would have been the wrong thing to do, he acknowledged fiercely. He would deal with her in the present and move on, all the stronger for the experience.

'Can I bring Harvey with me to the castle?' Ava

asked abruptly, realising that that would remove the dog from Marge's small overcrowded house.

Dark brows drawing together, Vito frowned, for his antipathy to indoor animals had only allowed him to stretch as far as a guinea pig and goldfish even for Olly.

'Honestly he won't be any trouble!' Ava promised feverishly, eager to persuade Vito round to her point of view. 'It's just Harvey will be put down if I can't find a home for him because Marge hasn't the room to keep him any longer. It'll buy him a little more time, that's all, and who knows? Someone may take a fancy to him on your estate.'

Vito surveyed Harvey, who was snoring loudly, re-markably relaxed for an animal apparently facing a sen-tence of death. He did not think he had ever seen a less prepossessing dog. 'Is he some peculiar breed?'

'No, he's a mongrel. He was a stray but he's young and healthy.' Ava gave him a tremulous, optimistic smile. 'He loves children too. He would be a great ad-dition to the party if I put a Santa hat on him…or maybe I could dress him up like a reindeer?'

Vito groaned out loud at the thought of more festive absurdity. 'Bring him with you if you like but don't get the idea that I'll keep him.'

'Oh, I would never expect that.' Ava laughed, re-leased from tension and weak with relief on Harvey's behalf. 'I'll keep him away from you. I know you're no good with dogs. Olly told me you were bitten when you were a child!'

Annoyance coursed through Vito and his eyes veiled, his jaw line hardening. He was an extremely private man. He wondered what other inappropriate revelations his little brother had made and once again he reflected that the sooner Ava was out of his workplace, the better.

'I'll have to get permission from my probation officer to leave London,' Ava told him suddenly, her expression anxious. 'I see her every month.'

'You'll only be away a couple of weeks—why bother mentioning it?'

'I'm out on parole, Vito. I have to follow the rules if I don't want to end up back inside,' she replied tightly.

Vito compressed his lips and gave an imperious nod of his handsome dark head in acknowledgement. 'I'll send a car to pick you up late Sunday afternoon.'

And then he was gone and the room felt cold and empty as if the sun had gone in. She sat down by the fire, all of a sudden cold on the inside as well and very shaky. What had she done? What madness had possessed her to agree to his proposition? The same madness that had made Vito Barbieri voice the suggestion? He wanted closure. She understood that, felt worse than ever when she thought about how hard it must have been for so reserved a male to deal with such a colossal tragedy. But on one level he was right—life went on whether you wanted it to or not and, just as he had done, she had to learn how to adapt to survive.

'I understand you'll only be here until Friday,' Karen Harper remarked sweetly the following morning as she checked over the typing that Ava had completed and sent her out to cover Reception over lunch. 'I had no idea just how friendly you were with the boss—'

'Friendly would be the wrong word,' Ava fielded awkwardly. 'Vito's still my boss.'

But the atmosphere around her for the rest of the

week was strained and she was in receipt of more nosy questions than she wanted to answer. It was a relief to leave early on Friday to keep her regular appointment with Sally, her probation officer.

'You'll be staying in a *real* castle?' Sally queried, goggle-eyed, as she made a note of the address.

'Not a medieval one—Bolderwood is a Victorian house,' Ava explained.

'And owned by Oliver Barbieri's brother,' Sally slotted in, smiling widely at Ava. 'He must be a very forgiving person.'

'No, he'll never forgive and forget where his brother's concerned and I don't blame him for that,' Ava replied tautly, her expression sober beneath the older woman's curious gaze. 'But he thinks we both need to get back to normal and he sees this as the best way of achieving that.'

'It's still a remarkably generous gesture.'

Travelling down to Bolderwood Castle two days later in the opulent luxury of a limousine with Harvey asleep at her feet and her holdall packed in the boot, Ava was thinking that she had never known that Vito possessed such a streak of generosity. But she should have done, she reasoned ruefully. Hadn't he given Olly a home when his kid brother was left alone in the world? A little boy he had only met a couple of times, a half-brother some adults might have thoroughly resented? Yet on the outside Vito Barbieri was as tough and inflexible as granite. In business he was as much feared as respected by competitors and at work—if AeroCarlton was anything to go by—his very high expectations and ruthless efficiency intimidated his employees.

As the familiar countryside passed the windows Ava grew increasingly tense. She was both terrified and ex-hilarated to be heading back to her childhood stomping grounds. Would she dare to visit her father or her sisters? She thought not, best not to push herself in rudely where she wasn't wanted. Her father and sisters would only resent her for turning up uninvited on their door-steps and putting them on the spot. Her eyes awash with moisture, she blinked back tears. She had to put her life back together alone but at least she still *had* her life.

'You have a very negative attitude,' Olly had once scolded her with his easy smile.

But then aside of his mother dying and his father having been an absentee parent, Olly had received a level of security, love and support from adults that Ava had never known. She knew that that was why she was prickly, suspicious of people's motives and always pre-pared for the worst. As the limo waited for the giant electric gates to open at the foot of the castle drive Ava's heart was in her mouth and she felt like scram-bling out of the car and running away. *Of course* peo-ple were going to think she was utterly shameless and insensitive to come and stay at Bolderwood after what she had done!

The car headlights illuminated the rambling Victorian mansion in the distance. Complete with four turrets and a forest of Elizabethan-esque chimneys, the original ar-chitect had recklessly borrowed the style of almost every previous age to embellish his creation. Ava had always thought it was a madly romantic house built in the days when owners had loads of staff and constantly enter-tained guests. Vito had a very large staff but kept the entertaining to the minimum. Throwing open the doors of his private home for the Christmas party was a major challenge for a male who happily lived behind locked gates and electric fences the rest of the year.

Eleanor Dobbs, the slim brunette housekeeper in her thirties, greeted Ava at the imposing front door. 'Miss Fitzgerald,' she said without an ounce of discomfiture. 'I'll show you straight up to your room so that you can get unpacked.'

'Just make it Ava,' Ava urged, her cheeks flushed with intense self-consciousness. 'How have you been?'

'It's been quiet here since your last visit,' the older woman remarked on her efficient passage up the sweeping staircase. 'We're all very pleased that the Christmas party is to be held again.'

A fixed smile on her taut face as she made determined small talk, Ava found herself standing in the principal guest room without quite knowing how she had arrived there. It was a massive room with a charming en suite bathroom in the turret complete with window seat. A fire burned in the grate of the marble fireplace, flickering shadows across warm brocaded walls and antique mahogany furniture. She stared in astonishment at the imposing four-poster bed draped in embroidered gold silk.

'Why have you brought me in here?' Ava whispered.

'Mr Barbieri asked me to prepare this room for you,' Eleanor advanced.

Ava froze. 'Where *is* Mr Barbieri?' she asked tightly.

'I believe he's in his bedroom.'

The housekeeper departed and Ava expelled her pent-up breath in a hiss while she scanned the opulence of the room. Totally unsuitable, she reflected incredulously. Vito could not put her in the main bedroom reserved for only the most honoured VIPs. My goodness, there was even a fire burning in the grate! Harvey, no slowcoach at spotting the most warm and comfy place in the room, settled down on the rug and lowered his shaggy head down on his paws.

'Don't bother getting comfortable,' Ava warned him ruefully. 'We're not staying in the five-star accommodation!'

Leaving Harvey, she crossed the landing at a smart pace to knock on Vito's bedroom door while she waited outside with folded arms. When there was no answer she knocked again and waited with mounting impatience. Finally she just opened the door and went in, only to stop dead on the threshold at the sight of Vito emerging from his en suite clad in only a pair of black briefs.

For a split second she simply stared, eyes wide, mouth dropping open in shock and awkwardness. He had an incredible body because he worked out and swam regularly in the basement fitness suite. Vibrant skin the colour of honey glowed in the lamplight, drawing attention to his powerful shoulders, truly remarkable abs and a stomach as flat as a washboard. Short black curls accentuated his pectorals while a silky dark furrow of hair ran down over his concave belly and disappeared below the waistband of his briefs. With her attention lingering in that most private area, embarrassment bit deep into Ava and she spun around, rejecting the view and presenting him with her back. 'I'm so sorry...I didn't mean to interrupt you—'

'At least close the door,' Vito said drily.

She shoved the door shut, her face so hot she thought eggs could have fried on it. What on earth had she been doing staring at him like that? As if she'd never seen a half-naked man before—she *hadn't*, though, apart from on the beach. Her lack of experience at almost twenty-two years of age affronted her pride. She was a case of arrested development, imposed by her years locked away in prison. Obsessed with Vito before she lost her freedom she had missed out entirely on the phase of youthful experimentation.

'*Che cosa a successo*...what has happened?' Vito drawled, cool as ice water with an edge of mockery.

Ava spun back to him, catching the sardonic hint of amusement written on his face as though on some level he relished her discomfiture. 'I came straight to find you because you simply can't plonk me in the main guest room!' she shot at him. 'It's a very bad idea.'

Engaged in drawing up the zip on a pair of close-fitting designer chinos, his magnificent torso providing a stunning display as his hips arched back and the ropes of muscle across his abdomen flexed, Vito had never looked more assured or calm. Being half naked in her presence clearly did not trouble him in the slightest. 'Let me decide what is appropriate,' he advised.

'Well, that's just it, isn't it?' Ava snapped back at him heatedly, inflamed by his refusal to take the subject seriously. 'Obviously I can't trust you to *do* what is appropriate!'

His black brows were level above his spectacular dark deep-set eyes. 'This is my house and I am the best judge of that. What I say goes here.'

His arrogant unconcern infuriated Ava. 'How can you completely ignore how other people will feel about me staying here?'

An ebony brow lifted. 'It's none of their business.'

'You have a hell of an attitude problem, Vito!' Ava hurled.

'Agreed,' Vito fielded softly as he reached for the shirt draped over the back of a chair. 'I never could stand being told what to do.'

The crack was not lost on Ava. She reddened, her lush mouth compressing. 'I'm not trying to tell you what to do—'

Vito studied her with interest, noting that she had chosen to travel in her office skirt and shirt, the violin curves above and below her tiny waist pronounced in the outfit. He wanted to rip the restrained garments off her, clothe her in excessively feminine silk and lace lingerie so that he could picture her lying on his bed without even stretching his imagination. Seeing her in his bedroom, he decided, was a disturbingly intimate experience.

'*Sì*, you are. You're a real little bossy-boots—you always were,' he riposted, watching her succulent lips part in surprise at the comeback, recognising the flare in her bright blue eyes with wicked anticipation.

Ava threw her head high, thick silky hair shimmering like a fall of molten copper round her cheekbones, eyes huge and fiery with defiance. 'I am *not* a bossy-boots!'

'Olly always did as he was told,' Vito murmured silkily. 'But be warned—I *don't*. You're in the main guest room purely because it was my decision to put you there.'

'Then put me somewhere a little more humble!' Ava cut in angrily.

In the strained silence that stretched in the wake of

her demand, the atmosphere hissed and buzzed like a crackling fire.

'No,' Vito responded, sliding a long arm smoothly into his shirt, his mind still engaged in imagining her on his bed seductively clad in little frilly bits of nothing. The pulse of urgency at his groin made him clench his teeth together. Desire, he recognised in exasperation, levelled all boundaries and defences.

'But I'm not an honoured guest here, I'm an employee!' Ava pointed out furiously. 'I should be staying in the staff quarters—'

'No,' Vito said again very quietly. 'I stand by my decision.'

'But it looks bad—'

Vito pulled on the shirt. 'You're a bright girl, Ava. Work it out for yourself.'

'Work what out?' Ava flung back at him in frustration. 'It's obvious that you can't treat me like a special guest without causing talk.'

Vito moved forward, the open shirt fluttering back from his strong muscled torso. 'Correct me if I'm wrong but didn't you spend three years in prison in punishment for your crime?'

Ava lost colour and her gaze dropped uneasily from his. 'Obviously I did.'

'So, you were tried and sentenced and you paid the price society demands. Where does it say that you have to go on paying?' he enquired impatiently. 'I put you in the principal guest room because if I treat you with respect everyone else will take their lead from me and award you the same level of respect.'

'It's not that simple,' she protested in a gruff undertone.

'It is,' Vito contradicted with serene confidence. 'Don't allow your insecurities to make it seem more complicated.'

A tempest of rage roared through Ava like a dam breaking its banks and she flung her head back, coppery hair dancing round her slim shoulders. 'I don't have insecurities!' she slammed back at him, defending the pride that was all she had left.

'Ava,' Vito countered very drily, 'you've always been a seething mass of insecurities.'

'That is not true…that is *so* totally untrue!' Ava hurled back at him tempestuously.

'*Madonna diavolo*…tell the truth and shame the devil,' Vito urged, lifting a hand and trailing a long finger mesmerically slowly along the length of her full lower lip.

Ava jerked her head back, startled by the tingle of awareness his touch ignited, which was already travelling straight to the heart of her body. 'Don't touch me…'

'You don't mean it,' Vito husked, shifting closer still to angle his handsome dark head down and lower his mouth to hers. 'You and I both know you don't mean it.'

CHAPTER FIVE

Vito settled a hand on the shallow indentation at the base of Ava's spine and tilted her forward into potent contact with his lean, powerful body. The heat and the ferociously physical feel of him against her shrivelled her defences, even before the hungry urgency of his mouth on hers blew them away completely. Locked to him, she swayed, knowing she had never dreamt that a kiss could make her feel so much. His pure passion called out to her and awakened a desperate craving for more.

She kissed him back eagerly, too worked up even to worry that her kissing might be of the amateur variety, too afraid that he might back off again as he had done twice before. As that subconscious fear penetrated she closed her arms round him, inviting, encouraging, no rational thought involved in the action. The piercing invasion of his tongue inside her mouth sent the blood racing like crazy through her veins and accelerated her heartbeat. Nothing had ever felt that necessary to her, nothing had ever felt that *right*.

'*Per l'amor di Dio,* Ava,' Vito growled against her mouth. 'You drive me crazy.'

'Is that bad?' Ava queried, stretching up on legs that

suddenly felt too short to plant a kiss against the un-smiling corner of his handsome mouth.

Vito twisted his head to capture her lips again with a deep groan that vibrated inside his powerful chest, big hands cupping her hips to force her closer so that she was sensually aware of his arousal. Involuntarily she rejoiced in his affirmation of her feminine power. The musky designer scent of him flared her nostrils and she shivered as he suckled her lower lip and the moist sweep of his tongue tangled with her own, other sensations that were yet more seductive taking charge of her as she pressed the tingling heaviness of her breasts into the hard wall of his chest.

She didn't feel the zip of her skirt going down, only registered its fall round her ankles a split second before he lifted her clear of its folds and brought her down on the bed. Boy, was that a smooth move, she thought help-lessly, just a little unnerved by such active proof of his experience and the fact that she was already on the bed without having decided to let him take her there. So, stop this now, stop acting like you can't control this, a dry little voice pronounced inside her confused head. A few kisses were one thing, more than that something else entirely. And although when she was younger she had often fantasised about occupying a bed with Vito in it, reality was a great deal more daunting. She could not forget Olly calling his big brother a predator with women. As Vito flipped off her shoes she sat up against the pillows and drew her knees up in a nervous ges-ture. Discarding his shirt, he came down on the foot of the bed and that fast, her troubled eyes drawn to his gleaming honey-coloured torso, she was lost to all common sense.

Her fingers spread across his warm flesh but he had his own ideas. He smoothed her slim legs flat and embarked on her shirt buttons, kissing her every time he released one. Air rushed in and out of her lungs and caught in her throat. She braced her hands on his satin-smooth shoulders. Her shirt vanished and with it her sensible cotton bra. He caressed the soft ripe swell of her breasts with appreciative hands, long fingers expertly teasing the throbbing peaks until a little moan escaped low in her throat. He took that as an invitation to dip his dark head and continue the delicious torment with his tongue. As he caressed her the tide of sensations rippled down her body and she felt an urgent heat building between her thighs.

'Don't stop touching me, *gioia mia*,' Vito urged, golden eyes smouldering with hungry appreciation as he looked down at her.

Colour flushed her cheeks and her fingers slid down over the tense muscles of his stomach and over the smooth cotton of his trousers to the hard bulge below. With a roughened exclamation, Vito released the button on his chinos and ran the zip down, his eagerness exciting her. Skimming the briefs out of her way with an unsteady hand, she ran an exploratory fingertip over his erection. He was velvet on steel, smooth and hard. While he lifted his hips every time she touched him it did not seem the right moment to consider the fact that there was a good deal more of him in that department than she had dimly expected. Ignorance pushed aside, because she was ready to learn from discovery, she bent her coppery head to take him in her mouth.

'No, I want you now,' Vito protested, drawing her up

to his level again to crush her generous mouth under his with erotic force. 'Is this what you want?'

Ava blinked, languorous blue eyes momentarily bemused. What *she* wanted? No problem answering that question and no hesitation for she suffered not a shade of doubt: him, absolutely only him. 'Yes...'

His fingers drifted down the long line of her slim thigh and she trembled, wanting, needing almost more than she could bear, wondering wildly if everyone felt every tiny caress so strongly and craved as much as she did. Or had the years she had spent shut away from the world made her rather more desperate? The thought shamed her, somehow forcing her to think of the caution she was abandoning. But then just once she wanted to go with the flow, experience rather than pre-plan. She gazed up at him, outwardly tranquil until she collided with the hot glitter of desire in his eyes. He was gorgeous. He was everything she wanted. How could she fight or deny what she was feeling?

'I love your body, *cara mia*,' he told her huskily. 'You're beautiful.'

In that moment he truly made her feel beautiful and she smiled dreamily, not believing but willing to credit that in the heat of passion she had magically acquired a special lustre in his eyes. As she watched him wrench off his chinos her heart began to beat very fast again. She didn't want to think and she tuned out her anxious thoughts but they broke through to the surface of her mind regardless, insisting on being heard. This was sex, nothing more to Vito, she reasoned reluctantly. She knew that, had to accept it. It never was anything more to him and she wasn't naïve enough to think that anything more than intimacy might come from it. The exhilarating spark of attraction that had always leapt between them was finally finding expression and it felt inevitable, something that would have happened no matter what she did.

Her panties seemed to melt away during another bout of heated kissing. She loved the taste and fire and strength of him. He stroked her soft, needy flesh below and she trembled as he slid a finger into her, while his thumb rubbed the madly sensitive little bead of her clitoris, making her tremble with delight.

'You're so wet…' he told her fiercely.

Shame engulfed Ava but she quivered as sensation drowned out everything in sweet waves she could hardly withstand in silence. Little whimpers escaped her throat in spite of her attempt to hold them back. She twisted as if she were in a fever, all control wrenched from her by the pleasure and the tormenting anticipation. He shifted away from her, leaving her body throbbing and pulsing with need and impatience. She heard the sound of foil tearing, knew he was donning protection and then he returned to her, rearranging her limbs with indisputable expertise. In one sure deep thrust he entered her and a choked cry of pain parted her lips, the sharp jab of discomfort unexpected and unwelcome.

Vito froze above her in shock, shaken dark golden eyes clinging to her hectically flushed face. 'I am the first?' he demanded in disbelief.

'Don't make a production out of it,' Ava urged, so embarrassed that she could not even meet his eyes. It hadn't occurred to her that it might hurt the first time. She hadn't thought about that aspect, had just lain back and expected nature to take its course, but possibly he was a little too passionate and well endowed for so relaxed an approach.

'How did you expect me to react?' Vito bit out, wildly disconcerted by what he had just learned about her. Ava, the teenager he had once deemed to be a seasoned little sexual temptress, was actually a virgin? That prospect had never crossed his mind once and he was not a man who liked surprises. Indeed he had an engrained distrust of surprises that came in a feminine package, life having taught him far too much about their hidden agendas.

'Well, it's done now,' Ava said baldly, refusing to cringe in mortification and mustering every ounce of her pride to her rescue. Evidently she wasn't the veteran of the sheets that he had assumed that she was and if he was disappointed he would just have to live with it.

'But why...*me*?' Vito growled suspiciously.

Ava angled up her hips to distract him and his broad shoulders tautened as he attempted to withdraw from the hot, tight embrace of her body. A second such movement from her became his undoing. He sank back into her enticing honeyed heat with a splintering groan of tortured desire and rage burned like a banked-down fire in his accusing gaze.

Ava evaded that look and shut her eyes. She had signed up for the whole experience, hadn't she? She wasn't about to allow him to wreck everything. Although did she really have any influence over Vito? Given the chance, it seemed he would have stopped, *rejected* her. Was virginity such a turn-off? Or was he afraid that her inexperience would prompt her to demand more from him than he was prepared to give? She had heard the old cliché that suggested virgins were more likely to become too attached to their lovers, seeking ties that went beyond the physical. That, she immediately sensed, was most likely what he feared. Well, he would soon discover that she cherished no such illusions where he was concerned.

'This isn't what I wanted,' Vito ground out.

'We don't always get what we want,' Ava pronounced woodenly, shifting her hips as a wonderful little tremor of devouring hunger and excitement shimmied up from her pelvis again like a storm warning. 'Don't spoil this....'

Torn between wanting to strangle her and wanting to keep her in bed for a week, Vito swore in his own language even as the natural promptings of his powerful libido took over. He had never wanted a woman as much as he wanted her at that moment but she felt like a guilty forbidden pleasure again. He didn't screw virgins, he didn't take advantage of inexperienced or vulnerable women.

Ava gave herself up to the pleasure, arching up in welcome to the enthralling glide of his body into hers. The ravenous excitement grew and grew as he thrust with simmering heat and strength and her body clenched and tightened round him, sending waves of exquisite sensation rolling through her body. His insistent rhythm quickened and her heart slammed inside her chest, the driving force of desire controlling her until at last she reached a quivering peak of spellbinding joy that spilled through her like an injection of happiness. Spasms of ecstasy were still rocking her when he shuddered over her in his own climax and she held him close, knowing she never wanted to let him go again but that she had to hide the fact.

'That was…different, *mia bella*,' Vito pronounced raggedly, pressing a slow measured kiss to her brow and then vaulting out of the bed to stride into the bathroom.

Ava breathed in slow and deep. She had revelled in that brief moment of togetherness but he had instantly shied away from that cosiness and she was not surprised; she was forewarned. *Different?* Not exactly a compliment she would queue up to receive, she acknowledged unhappily. As Vito reappeared she sat up, the sheet tucked beneath her arms, and said with deliberate carelessness, 'Different? It was just a bit of fun.'

An arrested expression froze his features, drawing her attention to the black shadow of stubble outlining his chiselled jaw and strong sensual lips. His eyes were as hard and bright as black diamonds between his screening lashes. '*Come ha detto?*…I beg your pardon?' he said levelly.

'The sex,' Ava murmured glibly. 'It was just a bit of fun, nothing you need to get worked up about.'

'You were a virgin!' Vito slammed back at her censoriously.

'And next week I'll be twenty-two-years old,' Ava informed him. 'How many twenty-two-year-old virgins do you know? It was past time I took the plunge.'

Already struggling with the turbulence of his emotions and a savage sense of guilt, Vito was inflamed by her reckless defiant attitude. Had he really believed her to be vulnerable? She talked as though she were coated in armour and she made it sound as though she had deliberately chosen him to deflower her. Furthermore she had reduced what they had shared to a basic meeting of bodies and, although on one level he accepted that that was what it had been, he could not subdue his angry sense of resentment. He had not meant to injure her in any way but he had made the crucial mistake of letting his high-voltage sex drive override his intelligence.

'I didn't look for the honour of becoming your first lover,' Vito spelt out with grim forbearance. 'In fact if I'd known I would never have touched you. I *assumed* you were experienced.'

Ava propped her chin on the heel of her hand, bright blue eyes misleadingly wide and calm, all anxiety and despondency suppressed for she refused to parade her true feelings in his presence. 'I am now,' she pointed out, high colour blooming over her delicate cheekbones as she made that claim.

'Casual sex is definitely not what you need right now,' Vito informed her with harsh biting conviction.

Her eyes veiled while she wondered how anything she did with him could be considered casual. Certainly not on her terms but on *his*? That was a very different matter. For Vito, sex could never have been anything else but casual with her. 'You don't know what I need— how could you? Look, give me something to wear so that I can return to my own room...'

Vito strode into the bathroom and emerged again to toss a black towelling robe on the bed. Her generous mouth arranged in a tight line of restraint, Ava dug her arms into the over-large garment and pulled it carefully round her to conceal her body before sliding out of the bed and knotting the sash at her waist. With fast-shredding dignity she stooped to pick up her discarded clothes and shoes, her heart like a crushed rock inside her weighing her down intolerably.

Ava shed the robe and stepped straight into the shower in her room. She was shell-shocked by what had happened between her and Vito Barbieri. Somehow, heaven knew how, her teenaged self had taken over her all-grown-up self and triumphed. Feeling the ache at the heart of her body, she grimaced and washed her body as roughly as someone trying to scrub their sins away with soap and water. When she was dry she pulled on jeans and a tee, fed the dwindling fire with a log and sat down beside it with Harvey. So, she had finally had sex and he had made it amazing but her emotions were in total turmoil. Idiot, she castigated herself as she smoothed Harvey's shaggy head and he rested back against her, brown eyes lovingly pinned to her tearstained face. I will not cry over Vito Barbieri, Ava told herself furiously. I made a mistake but *he* made a mistake as well.

She would act as if it had never happened, she decided in desperation. That was the only way to behave: as if it had been an inconsequential and meaningless episode she was keen to forget. She should never have gone to his bedroom, never have stood there shouting at him, challenging and provoking him. Just then the question of which room she occupied seemed unutterably trivial and not worth the fuss she had kicked up over it. Vito wasn't used to being challenged, she reminded herself ruefully. Vito dug in like a rock bedding down when you crossed him.

The knock on the door interrupted her thoughts. It was a maid with a tray.

'Mr Barbieri thought you might be hungry,' she explained, setting the tray down on an occasional table by the window and whisking the insulated cover off the plate.

'I could have come downstairs for it,' Ava said guiltily, looking down at the beautifully cooked chicken meal, her taste buds watering in spite of herself. As a teenager she had been downright uncomfortable at being served by the staff while she stayed at Bolderwood but now she was rather more practical in her outlook. Jobs at the castle were highly sought after because Vito paid well and offered good working conditions as well as apprenticeships in the key country skills still in demand on the estate.

'No need with a big staff and only two people to look after.' The girl laughed, clearly unfamiliar with Ava's past history with the Barbieri family.

Ava ate because she was indeed hungry and then she dug out a notebook and began to draw up a to-do list. Obviously calling the caterers came first and she would have to visit the garden centre that usually supplied the wreaths and garlands for the house. For the first time she wondered how she would get around because she had been banned from driving for the foreseeable future. Deeming that a problem better dealt with in daylight, she unpacked her holdall, which took all of five minutes. She took Harvey downstairs and, as directed by the housekeeper, she fed the dog in a rear hall before clipping on his lead and setting off through the solar-lit wintry gardens to take him for a brisk walk. The dim light was eerie, casting flickering shadows in the breeze with only the sound of her own feet crunching on the gravel paths in her ears. The whole place was just crammed with memories for her, she acknowledged painfully, for she could still remember sunbathing on the lawn and larking about with Olly while they studied for their final exams…the exams her friend had never actually got to sit. Ava had sat hers because her case had taken months to come to court. For most of

that period she had been away at school where she was
shunned like a leper for the tragedy she had caused and
when she had finally come home her welcome there had
proved even colder.

That night she slept in her comfortable bed, too ex-
hausted to be kept awake by her mental turmoil. When
she rose she was shocked to discover that it was almost nine, that she still felt tender in a certain place
and was in no mood to celebrate the loss of her virginity. Clad in her jeans, her trusty notebook in her back
pocket, she clattered downstairs with Harvey to take
care of his needs first. Eleanor Dobbs was waiting for
her when she came back indoors to direct her into the
dining room for breakfast.

'Could I have a word with you after you've eaten?'
she asked.

'Of course. Is Vito here?' Ava enquired stiffly, guessing that Eleanor wanted to discuss arrangements for
the party.

'The helicopter picks him up at seven most morn-
ings,' the older woman explained.

So, Vito was still locked into very early morning
starts, Ava reflected without surprise while she tucked
into cereal, fruit and coffee for breakfast. Work moti-
vated him as nothing else could and he didn't work because he needed more money either. Fabulously wealthy
though he was, Vito still worked virtually every day of
the week because he had once been the child of a spend-
thrift bankrupt and had lived through periods of great
insecurity. He had only put down permanent roots at
Bolderwood for Olly's benefit, recognising that the little
boy had needed a place he could call home.

Digging out her notebook before she even left the

dining room, Ava called the local caterers, who had provided the food and refreshments at the last party. She arranged a meeting for the following day and was heading up the stairs when the housekeeper appeared again.

'There's something I want to show you,' Eleanor told her uncomfortably. 'I thought maybe you could help.'

Ava lifted a fine brow. 'In any way I can,' she said evenly, wondering why the other woman was so tense.

Ava's tension mounted, however, when Eleanor Dobbs took her upstairs to what had once been Olly's room. She unlocked the door and spread it wide. Ava stood on the threshold in shock, for the room was untouched and looked as though it was just waiting for Olly to walk back in and occupy it. 'Why hasn't it been cleared?'

'I offered to do that soon after the funeral but Mr Barbieri said no. He used to come in here then but as far as I'm aware it's a couple of years since he did that.' The older woman grimaced. 'After all this time it just doesn't seem right to leave the room like this...'

Ava breathed in deep and straightened her shoulders. 'I'll sort it out,' she announced. 'Just bring me some boxes and bags and I'll go through all this stuff and decide what should be kept and stored. Then you can clear the room.'

'I'm very grateful,' Eleanor said ruefully. 'I didn't like to approach Mr Barbieri about it again. It's a sensitive subject.'

Alone again, Ava touched one of Olly's fossil specimens and tears swam in her eyes. Time had stood still within these walls, transforming the room into Vito's version of a shrine. That wasn't healthy, she thought painfully, recalling his speech to her about life going on.

The housekeeper helped her sort through Olly's pos-
sessions. Ava bagged his clothes for charity and put his
Harry Potter first editions, the fossil collection and his
photo albums into boxes. Leafing through the particu-
lar album that captured her two-year friendship with
Vito's brother, she laughed and smiled through her tears
as warmer less painful memories flooded back to her.
It was the first time she had allowed herself to recall
the good times they had had together and afterwards,
although she felt drained, she also felt curiously lighter
of heart.

When the job was complete she took Harvey out to
the garden where roses were still blooming in the mild
winter temperature and as she looked at those beautiful blooms an idea came to her and she went back indoors to get scissors. She had never got to say an official
goodbye to Olly, but she could now visit his grave and
pay her last respects without fear of offending anyone
as her appearance at his funeral would have done. Her
battered fake leather jacket zipped up against the breeze,
she left Harvey in Eleanor's care and walked out onto
the road, turning towards the small stone church little more than a hundred yards away. It had once been
part of the Bolderwood estate, having been built and
maintained by the original owners of the castle, but to
maintain his privacy Vito had provided separate access for the church.

A blonde woman climbing out of a sporty car parked
outside an elegant house opposite the church stared at
Ava with a frown as she opened the gate of the cemetery, which was surrounded by a low wall. Ava laid her
flowers down on Olly's grave, noting with a quivering

mouth that a stone angel presided over his final resting place: Olly had had great faith in angels.

'It *is* you, isn't it?' a sharp female voice exclaimed abruptly.

Ava spun round and recognised the blonde she had seen at the house across the road. She was very attractive, beautifully dressed in the sort of garments that shrieked their designer labels, and Ava felt very much at a disadvantage with her wan face and shabby clothing. A faint spark of familiarity tugged at the back of Ava's brain though and she surmised that she had seen the woman before. 'I'm sorry, I don't know you.'

'Why would you know me? I'm Katrina Orpington but we've never moved in the same social circles,' the blonde informed her scornfully. 'But I still know you— you're that Fitzgerald girl, the one who killed Vito's little brother! What on earth are you doing here at Oliver's grave?'

Chalk white though she was, Ava stood her ground. Her picture had been in the local paper a lot at the time of the court case and evidently she had been recognised. 'I just wanted to see where he was buried... It may be my fault that he died but he was my best friend,' she pointed out unhappily.

The blonde's lip curled with contempt. 'Well, I think your presence here is in very bad taste. Crocodile tears won't wipe out what you did. I'll never forget Vito's face that night—he was devastated!'

'Yes...I'm sure he was.' Ava's voice had shrunk to a mere whisper. 'But I can't change that and I didn't mean to offend anyone by coming here.'

'You have a thick skin and a lot of nerve, I'll give

you that!' the blonde pronounced, turning away to stalk back out of the cemetery.

Moisture stinging on her cheeks in the steadily cooling afternoon air, Ava went into the church and sat down on a rear pew, using the silence and sense of peace that churches always gave her to get a grip on her seesawing emotions. There was no escaping what she had done but she had to live with it, trust that she'd learned from it, hope that people would eventually stop seeing her as a killer and give her the opportunity to prove that she could be more than the sum total of her past sins. She thought of the previous night and cringed, deciding that she had sunk to slut level with Vito Barbieri, an unwelcome reading of the situation at a time when her spirits were already low. Feeling deeply vulnerable and alone, she said a prayer and then walked quickly back to the castle.

The afternoon flew by as Ava checked the rooms that would be used for the party and talked to the housekeeper about which pieces of furniture would need to be moved. Having made endless detailed lists and another couple of appointments, she was satisfied with her day's work. Apprehensive about being around when Vito came home, she took Harvey out for a long walk on the estate. A muddy Land Rover stopped beside her on one of the lanes and a tall blond man in his early thirties climbed out to introduce himself as the estate manager, Damien Skeel. It was wonderful to give her name to someone and see no awareness of her past in their response. Damien kept right on smiling at her, told her that his staff were delighted that the Christmas party was going ahead and urged her to contact him if she needed assistance with anything.

By then it was getting dark and Ava hastened home. She used the castle's rear entrance and straight away took care of feeding Harvey. She was about to head upstairs to freshen up when Eleanor Dobbs rushed through the green beige door that separated the main house from the kitchen wing, her face flushed and tense.

'Mr Barbieri is very angry that his brother's room was empty. It's my fault that it was done…I mean, I asked you to help. I told him that but I don't think he was listening,' she explained unhappily.

Ava stiffened. 'Oh, dear,' she muttered regretfully, suddenly wishing that she had never got involved.

'What the hell were you thinking of?' Vito roared at her as she crossed the hall a minute later and looked up to see him framed in the doorway of the library.

CHAPTER SIX

VITO was an intimidating sight. Still clad in a dark business suit teamed with a gold silk tie, he strode forward, his big broad shoulders blocking out the wall lights behind him. Ava had never quite appreciated how much taller he was than her until he stood in front of her, towering over her by a good nine inches, his face racked with condemnation.

Her breath rattled in her dry throat, a flush highlighting her pale complexion because it was the first time she had seen him since they had parted in his bedroom the previous evening and at that moment she was more conscious of that earlier intimacy than of her apparent offence. As she clashed with his hard gaze an utterly inappropriate tingle of erotic awareness spread through her body like poison. Vito grabbed her wrist and pulled her into the library, where he shut the door behind them.

'*Per meraviglia!* What were you thinking of?' he demanded a second time, his Italian accent giving every word with a growling edge. 'I came home, noticed the door was open…saw the room stripped. I couldn't believe my eyes! Who, I wondered, could possibly have the colossal nerve and insensitivity to go against my wishes in my own home?'

While he spoke, his breath fracturing audibly with the force of his wrath, his eyes hot and bright with outrage, Ava hastily thought of, and discarded, several possible responses in favour of simple honesty. 'I thought it was for the best—'

'*You* thought?' Vito erupted with incredulous bite. 'What the hell has it got to do with you?'

'Obviously I should have asked you about what you wanted done first,' Ava declared shakily, for she had never dreamt that her intervention might rouse such a reaction.

'It was none of your business!' Vito glowered at her in a tempestuous fury she had not known he was capable of experiencing. He was in such a rage that he could hardly get the words out and she knew that he was finding it a struggle to voice his feelings in English rather than Italian.

'I thought I understood how you felt. Obviously I was mistaken but I honestly believed that clearing the room would make you feel better,' Ava protested tautly.

'How the hell could a bare room make me feel better? It's simply another reminder that Olly's gone!' Vito ground out bitterly while treating her to a burning look of fierce rage.

Was that rage directed at her as the driver of the car that awful night? As she couldn't blame him if that was the underlying source powering him, her shoulders slumped. 'I didn't get rid of the personal stuff. His collections and photos and books and letters were all boxed up and kept,' Ava told him eagerly.

Vito snatched in a ragged breath, his mouth settled into a tough, contemptuous line. 'I want it all put back... exactly as it was!'

Ava straightened her slim shoulders, her bright blue eyes deeply troubled by that instruction. 'I don't think that's a good idea—'

'*You* don't think?' Vito's deep drawl scissored over the words like a slashing knife. 'What has it got to do with you? Did seeing that room empty of Olly make you feel guilty? Is that what your invasion of my privacy is really all about?'

'Yes, seeing his room again made me feel guilty and very sad. But then even being in this house makes me feel guilty. But I'm used to feeling like that and it didn't influence my decision.'

'Your decision?' Vito derided with positive savagery, his voice raw with aggrieved bitterness. 'You *killed* my brother. Was that not enough for you? What gave you the insane idea that desecrating his room and my memory of him would make me feel better?'

At that lethal reminder, spoken to her by him for the first time, Ava flinched as though he had struck her. The blood slid away from below her skin, leaving only sick pallor in its wake. He had the right to hate and revile her: who could deny him that outlet when he had never before confronted her on that score? Her tummy filled with nausea and an appalling sense of shame and guilt that she knew she could do nothing to assuage.

'I was unforgivably high-handed...I can see that now,' Ava admitted jerkily, pained regret slicing through her that she could have been that thoughtless and inconsiderate. Unfortunately she had always been quick to act on a gut reaction and think about consequences later and this time it had gone badly wrong for her. 'But I honestly wasn't thinking about how *I* felt when I cleared the room. I was thinking about you.'

'I don't want you thinking about me!' Vito roared as he strode across to the decanter set on the sofa table and poured himself a shot of whiskey. 'My thoughts and feelings about my brother's death are entirely my affair and not something I intend to discuss.'

'Yes, I have got that message but that locked-up untouched room didn't strike me as a healthy approach to grief,' Ava dared to argue, her attention resting on the rigid angles and hollows of his strong face and the force of control he was clearly utilising to hide his feelings. He was as locked up inside as that blasted room, she thought in sudden frustration, but it was a revelation to her that he possessed the depth that fostered such powerful emotions.

'What would you know about it?' Vito slashed back at her rudely, for once making no attempt to hide how upset he was, which she found oddly touching.

'I've been through something similar and talking about it or even writing about it for purely your own benefit helps,' she murmured ruefully. 'Grief can devour you alive if you get stuck in it.'

He skimmed her with cutting emphasis. 'Spare me the platitudes! And don't ever interfere in my life again!'

'I won't, but remember that it was *you* who told me that you can't live in the past for ever and that life has to go on,' Ava reminded him wretchedly. 'I'm sorry if I misinterpreted what you meant by that. I thought I was helping.'

'I don't need or want your help!' Vito slammed at her in a wrathful fury as he wrenched open the library door again. 'Tell Eleanor I'm eating out tonight!'

And Ava was left standing there in the pool of light by the desk. She gritted her teeth. She was hurting, Vito was hurting but he didn't want anyone, least of all her, to recognise the fact. That wounded her but she had no right to feel wounded because she *had* been insensitive not to broach the topic of clearing Olly's room with him personally.

A soft knock sounded on the door and Ava moved forward to open it. 'Vito said—'

'Don't worry, I heard him,' Eleanor confided with a grimace and she winced as the sound of a powerful car tearing down the drive carried indoors. 'I hope you told the boss that clearing that room was *my* idea.'

'I encouraged you and I got stuck in first. I thought it was the right thing to do as well. Forget about it,' Ava advised.

Eleanor frowned. 'I've never seen Mr Barbieri lose his temper like that. Should I start putting the room back the way it was?'

'I would wait and see how he feels about it tomorrow…but maybe listening to my opinion isn't the right way to go,' Ava pointed out heavily, reaching down to fondle Harvey's ears as he bumped against her knee.

'Harvey's got a lovely nature,' the housekeeper remarked in the awkward silence. 'I'll spread the word about him needing a home but, if you ask me, he's already happy to have found a home with you.'

'But pets aren't allowed where I live in London,' Ava muttered, struggling to concentrate when all she could hear, over and over again in her buzzing head, was Vito saying, 'You killed my brother.' And she *had*, not deliberately but through recklessness and bad judgement. That was a truth she had to live with, but just then acknowledging it wounded her as much as it had the day in hospital when she had first learned that Olly had died in the crash.

Ava had no appetite for the delicious evening meal brought to her in the solitary splendour of the dining room. After rooting through Vito's library to find a Jane Austen novel she hadn't read in several years, she went for a swim in the basement, desperate to escape her unhappy thoughts. Afterwards, the warmth and privacy in her bedroom along with Harvey's relaxing presence enclosed her. Momentarily she remembered how noisy prison had been and how comfortless, with metal furniture fixed to the wall and a tiny floor space with only a view of another prison block out of the small window. Bells had rung sounding out meal times and exercise periods, barred gates had clanged and sometimes alarms had gone off as well. Pounding music had been an almost constant backdrop while other inmates shouted from cell to cell, bored silly at being locked up for so many hours a day. She shivered. The first two years she had had to struggle to get through every day but she had eventually settled into a routine. She had found work helping others to read and write and had learned to appreciate tiny things like the right to buy a hot chocolate drink or a snack with her meagre earnings. She had also learned very fast to stop feeling sorry for herself because there were so many others dealing with much worse stuff than she had on her plate.

Recalling that stark reality, Ava decided to run a bath in the opulent turret room en suite and luxuriate in the selection of bathing products available. Staying at the castle was very much like staying at a five-star hotel. It was a luxury holiday and she ought to make the most of it because reality would soon be back loudly knocking at her door again, she reminded herself impatiently. But she felt so horribly guilty about having wounded Vito by forcing him to face up to his half-brother's death all over again. She had trod in hobnail boots all over his sensibilities by foolishly underestimating his attachment to the picture of the past that could still flourish in that locked room. He was right. Who was she to say it was healthy or otherwise to leave that room as though time had stopped dead?

Ava wasted a lot of time lounging in the decadent bath, topping up the water to warm it when she got cold, fighting with all her might to escape her unhappy thoughts. She had screwed up again and she clenched her teeth hard and tried again to blank her mind. She donned her pyjamas, blew dry her hair and set her mobile phone alarm to wake her up early. But *not* early enough to run into Vito as she was convinced that he wouldn't want to share the breakfast table with her. She took Harvey out for a last run before clambering into her comfortable bed to read until she got sleepy.

When the door opened rather abruptly, Harvey leapt up and barked and Ava sat up with a start. Just about the very last person she was expecting walked in, leaning back against the door to close it. Harvey barked again, tense with suspicion at the interruption. Ava leant out of bed to soothe him into silence and he subsided and slunk back to his favourite spot by the dying fire.

'I saw the light from outside and realised you were still awake,' Vito informed her as she glanced at her watch to note that it was after eleven. 'Damien gave me a lift home from the village pub.'

Absolutely flummoxed by his appearance in her bedroom wearing nothing more than his boxer shorts—his towelling robe was, after all, still lying in a heap on her floor—with his hair still tousled and damp from the shower, Ava was as tense as a bowstring but trying against all the odds to act normally. 'Oh, yes, I met Damien when I was out walking today and he introduced himself. He's very friendly.'

His face tensed, his eyes narrowing with laser precision. 'Was he flirting with you?'

'Possibly,' Ava responded tactfully, because Damien had been flirting like mad with her during their brief conversation, even confessing to her that young single women were scarcer than hens' teeth in the neighbourhood and that he had started attending the church services in the hope of meeting more people, only to discover that the greater part of the congregation was as old as the hills.

'I'll warn him off…I don't share,' Vito delivered darkly.

Ava blinked. 'You really don't need to warn him off.'

'I don't do one-night stands either,' Vito continued with lashings of assurance.

In the act of dragging her eyes from his truly magnificent physique, Ava blushed like a tongue-tied adolescent and could think of absolutely nothing to say to that when he was clearly, in spite of their earlier difference of opinion, planning to spend the night with her.

'But I think, right now, I could be very much into fun, *bella mia*,' he confided raggedly, the tough front lurching slightly.

'I don't know how to do casual,' Ava told him jerkily, her nerves getting the better of her vocal cords but the sting of his reproof about casual sex unforgotten.

'I don't either,' Vito murmured silkily, tossing something down on the bedside cabinet and throwing the duvet back and climbing into the bed beside her as though he slept with her every night and it were the most normal thing he could do.

'Vito…' Ava began in a troubled voice.

Vito ran a finger caressingly down the length of her slender throat to rest where a tiny pulse was beating out her tension below her collarbone. Hot golden eyes looked levelly into hers. 'I don't want to sleep alone tonight.'

'Oh,' Ava said stupidly, but in truth she was transfixed by the admission from such a source. Vito, who needed no one, listened to no one and who never confessed to human weakness was telling her something she had never expected to hear from him. He wanted— no, *needed*—to be with her and he could not have said anything more calculated to appeal to her.

He brushed his lips very gently across hers, his breath fanning her cheek. 'Do you want me to leave?'

Ava froze at the offer. 'Er, no—'

'But hopefully you don't want me to stay because you wanted me at eighteen and couldn't have me?' he pressed, evidently concerned that that might be the case.

He was asking her to divorce the past from the present and she wasn't sure she could do that. 'I just want you,' Ava said gruffly, shorn of her usual cool. 'But I assure you that I got over my obsession with you at eighteen.'

'I don't like the idea that I'm taking advantage of you,' Vito admitted grimly. 'Here I am, I'm not drunk but I'm not sober either, and I'm not even thinking about what I'm doing.'

'That's OK, no big deal,' Ava soothed softly, patently

unaware of how rare it was for Vito to do anything without thinking it through first. 'It's not important.'

'I'm not about to fall in love with you and marry you or anything like that!' Vito warned her, derision at the idea giving his mouth a sardonic twist. 'This is an affair, nothing more complex. Don't overthink it.'

'I never thought I would say it but you talk too much,' Ava told him with sudden amusement. 'I'm not that daft dreaming teenager you remember—I grew up and I'm not even twenty-two yet. I don't want to get married for years and years and years!'

'I don't *ever* want to get married,' Vito traded, throwing himself back against the pillows while wondering how he could possibly be irritated by her total lack of interest in marrying him. Naturally that was good news and she was blessedly free of the carefully presented hypocrisies with which his more usual style of lover sought to set him at his ease. Of course she was ten years younger than he was and that was a fair gap, he acknowledged, tension filtering through his momentary relaxation. In fact it was almost cradle-snatching.

Ava leant over him, her hair brushing a big shoulder while she marvelled at the conversation they were having. 'I don't want to marry you. I want to play the field and have fun first.'

'If Damien Skeel comes on to you, you tell me,' Vito spelt out rawly in a knee-jerk reaction that shook him because it seemed to come from some strange place inside him he didn't recognise. 'And you're not going to be playing the field and having fun with anyone but me until we're over. Is that understood?'

A pang pierced Ava. She didn't like to hear him talk of their affair being over before it had even really begun.

It hurt, just as breaking up would hurt, she reminded herself impatiently. She wasn't a kid any more. She didn't cherish a little soap bubble fantasy of Vito falling madly in love with her and sweeping her down the aisle to an altar. Even as a teenager she had not been that naïve.

'Do you always lay down the law in bed like you're in the boardroom?' Ava teased.

'I need to with you. You're a new and very original box of tricks, *cara mia*,' Vito contended, pushing her playfully flat against the pillows to extract a long, drugging kiss that sent her heartbeat into overdrive.

She felt tiny beneath him, crushed by his broad chest and the hair-roughened thigh that had slid between hers. She was madly aware of her nipples tightening into tingling buds and of the hard press of his arousal against her. He wanted her. For a split second she simply luxuriated in that sweet wonderful knowledge. She wanted him and he wanted her. Finally, the time was right. And then in dismay she recalled the rather childish tattoo on her hip and resolved to buy some large plasters as soon as she could to conceal that revealing marking before he could see it. He wouldn't think of her as an adult for long if he caught a glimpse of that.

Vito sat up and tossed back the duvet. 'What on earth are you wearing?' he demanded.

'My PJs.'

'Gingham just isn't sexy,' Vito pronounced with authority and embarked on the buttons.

Ava lay there stiff with embarrassment while he stripped off her pyjamas and reminded herself that he had seen it all before and that it was silly to feel so self-conscious. 'Put the light out,' she still urged him.

'No…you're a work of art and I want to savour you,' Vito countered without hesitation, studying the long svelte line of her pale body. 'I was in far too much of a hurry yesterday.'

'I'm cold,' she told him, hauling up the duvet at speed again.

'No, you're shy and I never realised that before. Ava Fitzgerald…*shy*,' Vito commented with rich amusement. 'Wow…you've turned as pink as a lobster.'

'If you refer to lobsters and me in the same sentence again you can go back to your own room!' Ava hissed vitriolically, blue eyes sparkling like sapphires in her elfin face.

'It's not happening.' With a sudden laugh, Vito crushed her mouth beneath his again, his tongue delving deep in a devouring kiss that sent erotic thrills coursing through her all too ready body. When he discarded his rigid self-discipline and reserve, there was so much passion pent-up inside him, Ava thought, thrilled by his approach.

His mouth closed over the swollen peak of her breast and she shivered as he tasted and teased her with his tongue. The glide of his teeth followed and she moaned, startled and aroused, the heat at the heart of her beginning to build. Her hips arched and he stilled her.

'We're going to do this right this time, *bella mia*,' Vito informed her, his exotically handsome features taut with determination.

'*Right?*' Ava repeated in disbelief. 'Keep the control freakiness for the office.'

'I am not a control freak,' Vito growled.

He *so* was. Ava cupped his face and connected with smouldering golden eyes that made her heartbeat hammer. He was beautiful. She just loved looking at him, and then he kissed her again with that sensual full mouth and the ability to think fell away. As he began to lick and kiss his way down over her body her hands dug into his shoulders and suddenly it was a challenge to breathe. She thought he might be going to do...*that*, not something she could imagine doing with anyone, not even him. She tried to urge him back up again but either he failed to take the hint or he deliberately put himself out of reach.

'Vito...I don't think I want that,' Ava muttered tightly.

'Give me a one-minute trial,' Vito purred, settling hot, hungry eyes on her. 'While you think about it.'

Already pink, Ava could feel herself turn hot red and she just closed her eyes, not wanting to be inhibited and a turn-off. His hands smoothed over her thighs and eased them apart. I'm not going to like this but I'll put up with it, she decided, and then he touched her with his tongue on the most super-sensitive part of her body and she almost leapt in the air at the sensation. He made a soothing sound deep in his throat that she found incredibly sexy. Slow-burning pleasure turned to raw ecstasy incredibly fast and she went wild, gasping and rising off the bed as an explosive climax engulfed her. Dazed by it, she felt limp as he shifted over her and sank into her hard and fast. Nothing had ever felt as intense. Her body had discovered a new level of sensitivity and in its already heightened state, his rapid powerful movements swiftly awakened the throbbing heat and hunger of need again.

'*Porca miseria!* You make me wild!' Vito panted.

Her every sense was on hyper alert and excitement

as she had never known was clawing at her. She didn't
have the breath to respond. Her fingers raked down his
back over his flexing muscles as she reacted to sensations as close to pleasure as torment, wanting more,
wanting, her entire body reaching as her back arched
and the glorious splintering high peak of blinding pleasure engulfed her again as a shrill cry was wrenched
from her.

'On a scale of one to ten that was a twenty,' Vito
husked in her ear. 'I'm sorry, I was rough—'

'I liked it,' Ava mumbled in a forgiving mood, both
arms wrapped round him, happiness dancing and leaping through her limp, satiated body like sunlight on a
dull wintry day.

'You're miraculous, *gioia mia*,' Vito said thickly, an
almost bemused look in his stunning dark eyes as he
bent down awkwardly and dropped a kiss on her nose.
But he then freed her from his weight and proximity
so fast that her hands literally trailed off him and she
half sat up in surprise as he strode into the bathroom.
He had used contraception, she reminded herself diz-
zily. Miraculous? Was that good? Her mind was full of
words like, 'astonishing, magnificent, unbelievable'.
Even so, she wished he hadn't left her so suddenly. As
that thought occurred to her Vito reappeared and swept
up his robe to put it on. Ava blinked. He wasn't coming
back to bed? Perhaps he was hungry.

Vito had got halfway to the door before Ava spoke.
'Where are you going?'

'To bed.' Vito half turned back to her, a brow slightly
quirked as though he wondered why she was asking
such an obvious question of him.

Such fury shot through Ava that she felt light-headed

with it. 'Oh, so that's it for tonight, is it? Having got what you wanted, you just walk out on me?'

Vito swung all the way round and levelled stunned dark eyes on her. 'I always sleep in my own bed…it is not meant as an insult or any kind of statement.'

'You mean you *never* spend the night with anyone?' Ava prompted, utterly disconcerted by the news.

'I like my privacy,' Vito admitted a shade curtly, unable to understand why she was complaining when no other woman ever had.

'Well, you can have all the privacy you want from me,' Ava snapped back at him. 'But let me make one thing clear—if you walk through that door you don't get back in again on any pretext!'

His eyes shimmered and narrowed, his face tensing with the surprise and considerable hauteur of a male unaccustomed to any form of rejection from a woman. 'You can't be serious.'

'That's the way it is, Vito. Take it or leave it. I thought the practice of *droit de seigneur* went out with the Crusades and you're not going to treat me like a late-night snack and get away with it!' Ava slung tempestuously as she punched a pillow, doused the light to leave him poised in darkness and lay down again.

Vito opened the door, hesitated—*fatally*, he later realised. He thought of waking up beside Ava. He shed his robe where he stood.

As Ava felt the mattress give beneath his weight she thought about the power of 'miraculous' sex over a male and it made her want to punch him more than ever. He was spoilt by too much money and too many eager-to-please women.

'Am I expected to cuddle as well?' Vito enquired with sardonic bite.

'If you value your life, stay on your own side of the bed,' Ava advised bluntly.

Silence fell, a silence laden with nerve-racking undertones. Ava grimaced in the darkness and wished she had kept quiet. You could lead a horse to water but you couldn't make it drink, she reminded herself wryly, a situation not improved by the fact that he was stubborn as a mule. He didn't do the cuddly sleeping-together stuff but she didn't think she could do an affair without affection at the very least. Who are you kidding? she asked herself. She was only at the castle for another two weeks and the minute the party was done, she would be history. She needed to learn how to take each day as it came just the way she had done in prison, but there was no way on earth that she would live according to *his* rules alone.

'I shouldn't have lost my temper with you about Olly's room,' Vito mused very quietly.

'I shouldn't have gone ahead and touched it without speaking to you about it first,' Ava traded, her stiffness receding a little.

'I used to go in there and sit in the months after the funeral,' Vito volunteered curtly. 'Fortunately I managed to wean myself off that habit, so there was no reason to leave the room the way it was while he was alive.'

Ava gritted her teeth and bit back hasty words because Vito was a stiff-upper-lip kind of male. 'Why should you have had to wean yourself off going in there?' she finally asked. 'There was no harm in it if it gave you comfort.'

'It was a weird thing to do,' Vito asserted in a tone

that warned her that he expected her to agree with him on that score.

Ava suffered a truly appalling desire to hug him but she imagined him shaking her off and didn't move a muscle in his direction. 'No, it wasn't weird. It was completely natural. He was on your mind. You didn't need to fight off the urge as if it was wrong. You're just terrified of feeling emotion, aren't you? But all you did was make it harder for yourself.'

'I am not terrified of feeling emotion!' Vito grated in disbelief.

Ava begged to disagree in silence. Macho man had not been able to cope with the threatening desire to sit in his kid brother's room occasionally and quite typically he had walled his grief up inside himself, convinced that that was the best way.

'I'm *not*,' Vito repeated doggedly, wondering why he had conversations with her that he never had with anyone else while trying to recall emotional moments without success.

Ava smiled and went to sleep.

CHAPTER SEVEN

FLOWERS would be old-fashioned, Vito reasoned five days later, during a boardroom meeting at his London headquarters that he was finding unbelievably tedious. He had another five hours to put in before he could call it a day. Impatient, he glanced at the wall clock again while his mind wandered to picture Ava clad in sexy lingerie reclining on his bed and then immediately discarded the fantasy. Unlike most of his past lovers, she would hit the roof if he gave her a gift like that. *What am I? Your little sex toy?* So attuned had he become to Ava's feisty take on life, he could actually *hear* her saying it. No, definitely not the lingerie. What did you give a woman who acted as if your millions didn't exist? Chocolate? Boring, predictable. Exasperation sizzled through his tall, powerful physique. He could not recall ever expending this much mental energy on anything so trivial. What did she need? Clothes. Ava was the proud possessor of the very barest of necessities. But she wouldn't like him buying her clothes either. His big shoulders squared, his strong jaw line clenched. *Dio mio*, she would just have to put up with it.

'Mr Barbieri…?'

Vito focused on the speaker with a blankness of mind

he had no prior experience of in a business setting. He wondered if he was ill. Maybe he had the flu, maybe he had allowed himself to get too tired. Yes, that was it, too much sex, not enough rest, he decided, relieved by the explanation but acknowledging that he was not about to change his ways...not with Ava under his roof. He stood up lithely and offered his apologies for his sudden departure while explaining that he had some-where else to be.

That same day, Ava made her decision over breakfast: she would go and see her father. It was a Saturday and the older man always liked to stay home and read the papers in the morning.

Fear of rejection, nerves and guilt had kept her from the door of her former family home, she acknowledged ruefully. Her court case and prison sentence along with the newspaper articles written about her fall from grace had seriously embarrassed her family and her father, who worked as a member of Vito's accounting team, had been convinced that her role in Olly's death had en-sured that he was passed over for promotion. For those reasons, she was certainly not expecting a red carpet rolled out for her but she wanted to say sorry and dis-cover if there was any way of restoring some kind of bond with her relations. If it crossed her mind that there never had seemed to be much of a bond between her and them, she suppressed the thought and concentrated on thinking positively.

The past week had proved incredibly busy but all the party arrangements were running smoothly and she had begun to decorate the house. She tried not to think too much about Vito while she was working. After all, in less than a week's time she would be leaving and the affair would be over. That was *not* going to break her heart, she told herself firmly, but the hand in which she held her cup of coffee trembled. Hastily she set the cup down again. If she gave way to stupid feelings, started fancying that she was in love and all that nonsense she would be digging her own descent into despair by the time it ended. And no man was allowed to have that much power over Ava because in her experience, with the single exception of Olly, the people she loved had always hurt her badly. No, just as Vito didn't do marriage, Ava didn't do love.

Admittedly she was attached to him in some ways, she acknowledged grudgingly. He kept on trying to take her out to dinner and places which she hadn't expected, having assumed he would be as keen as her to keep their involvement with each other under wraps. Certainly the staff must have guessed but by the time such rumours spread further afield Ava would be long gone. She had told Vito she had nothing to wear that wouldn't embarrass them both in public but it was just an excuse to hide the fact that she didn't want people to know they were involved. Much wiser to stay under the radar, she reflected ruefully, having no desire to attract controversy or see Vito outraged or upset by people who would be appalled that he could have fallen into bed with the woman responsible for his brother's death. That was life and Ava had learned not to fight it.

Vito and her? It was just sex, she told herself every time he was with her. He couldn't keep his hands off her but, to be honest, she couldn't keep her hands off him either and the awareness that they had such a short time together had simply pushed the intensity to a whole new level. He was with her every minute he was at home and, although he was characteristically working on a Saturday, he had gradually started finishing earlier and earlier. They argued at least once a day, being both very strong-willed people. But they never let the sun go down on a row either and he stayed with her every night, dragging her up to breakfast with him at an unforgivably early hour while striding through the castle shouting for her if she wasn't immediately available when he arrived home. She knew he liked her and that he cared about what happened to her. She respected his fair-mindedness, was even fond of him. But aside of the wild bouts of sex that took place every time they got within touching distance, that was the height of it, she told herself staunchly. With six days of the affair to go, she believed she was handling the upcoming prospect of their separation with logic and restraint rather than with the obsessive depth and despondency that would once have threatened her composure. After all, hadn't that obsessional passion of hers for Vito once sent her running out of control into that car with tragic consequences? She knew better now.

The neat detached home that Ava's parents had brought her up in sat behind tall clipped hedges on the outskirts of the village. Even though it was two miles from the castle, Ava walked there. Damien Skeel had been instructed to put a car and driver at her disposal to facilitate the party arrangements but Ava didn't want an audience to witness her being turned away from her father's front door. As smartly dressed as she could contrive, she braced herself and rang the doorbell.

She was bewildered when a stranger answered the door and wondered in dismay if her father had moved house after her mother's death. 'I'm looking for Thomas Fitzgerald,' she said to the middle-aged blonde woman. 'Has he moved?'

'I'm his wife. Who should I tell him is here?' the woman responded.

Ava's eyes widened as she tried to hide her shock that her father had remarried. 'I'm his youngest daughter, Ava.'

'Oh.' The polite smile dropped away and the older woman turned her head hurriedly and called out, 'It's... *Ava*!'

Her father appeared from the direction of the kitchen, a tall thin man with grey hair and rather cold blue eyes. 'I'll deal with this, Janet. Ava...you'd better come in,' he said without any sign of warmth.

But an invite to enter her former home was still more than Ava had expected after having her existence ignored for three long years, and her tension eased a tiny bit. True, it was a shock that her father had already taken a second wife but she had no resentment of the fact because her parents had never been happy together. The older man showed her into the dining room and positioned himself at the far side of the table, distancing tactics she was accustomed to and which felt dauntingly familiar.

'I suppose you want to know what I'm doing here.' Ava spoke first, used to the older man's power play of always putting her in that position.

'If you're hoping for a handout you've come to the wrong place,' Thomas Fitzgerald informed her coldly.

'That's not why I came, Dad. I've served my sentence—that's all behind me now and, although I know I caused a lot of trouble for the family, I...' Ava paled and struggled to find the words to express her feelings in the face of the look of icy distaste that her father wore.

'I suppose you were sure to turn up like the proverbial bad penny sooner or later,' he pronounced drily. 'I'll keep this short for both our sakes. I'm not your father and I have no obligation towards you.'

Ava felt as if the floor had dropped away below her feet. '*Not*…my father?' she repeated thickly, incredulous at the statement. 'What are you talking about?'

'While your mother was alive it was a secret but thankfully there's no need for that nonsense now,' he told her with satisfaction. 'My wife and your half-sisters are aware of the fact that you're not a real member of this family. Your mother, Gemma, picked up a man one night and fell pregnant by him. And *no*, I know nothing about who he was or is and neither did your mother, who was…as usual…drunk.'

'Picked up a man?' Ava echoed, her pallor pronounced and a sick feeling curdling in her stomach.

'Yes, it's sordid but that's nothing to do with me. I'm telling you the truth as your mother finally told it to me,' Thomas Fitzgerald continued with open distaste. 'You were DNA tested when you were seven years old and my suspicions were proven correct. You are *not* my child.'

'But nobody ever said anything, even suggested that…' Ava began jerkily, trying and failing to get her freefalling thoughts into some kind of order and comprehend the nightmare that seemed to be engulfing her. 'Why didn't you divorce my mother?'

'What would have been the point of a divorce?' the older man asked with unhidden bitterness. 'She was an alcoholic and I had two daughters, whom I couldn't have trusted her to raise alone, *and* I had my career. I didn't want people sniggering about me behind my back either. I tried to make a go of the marriage in spite of you. I was a decent man. I fed and clothed you, educated you, did everything a father is expected to do...'

Momentarily, it was as though a veil had fallen from Ava's perceptive powers as she looked back at her childhood and adolescence. 'No, you didn't. You never liked me.'

'How was I supposed to like you?' he shouted at her in a sudden eruption of rage. 'Some stranger's bastard masquerading as my own daughter? It was intolerable that I should be forced to pretend but I was responsible for your mother because I married her. There was no one else to take care of her and I had to think of Gina and Bella's needs. I did my duty by you all but it was a lot more than your wretched mother deserved!'

The door behind Ava opened. 'Thomas, I think you've said enough,' the female voice said quietly. 'It's not the girl's fault that you had to put up with so much.'

It was his wife, Janet, *her* stepmother...no, not her stepmother. These two people were actually no relation to her at all. The shock of that realisation punched through Ava and left a big hole where she felt her brain should be. She turned in a clumsy circle. 'I should leave.'

'I think that would be best, dear. You remind Thomas of a very unhappy time in his life,' Janet informed Ava in a reproachful tone.

Ava walked straight back out onto the road, feeling as if she had concussion because she couldn't think straight. The secret was out: she finally knew why her father had never liked her and her mother had always preferred her sisters. Evidently she was 'some stranger's bastard', not a legitimate child of Thomas Fitzgerald's first marriage, not to mention being a constant galling reminder of his wife's infidelity. No longer did she need to wonder why the man had persisted in calling her 'Ginger', why she had been sent off to school, shunned and excluded from the family when she messed up: she wasn't a part of the family and was barely entitled to call herself by the name Fitzgerald. All her life she had been a cuckoo in the nest and now she knew why and there was absolutely nothing she could do about it. No amends that she could make, no bridges she could possibly build. The family reunion she had prayed for was nothing more than a silly girlish pipe dream.

Vito flew back to the castle in his helicopter, warned the pilot he would be returning to London within the hour and strode from the helipad towards the front door. There he spotted Damien Skeel lounging up against the bonnet of his four-wheel estate vehicle and he frowned.

'I suppose you don't happen to know where Ava is?' Damien asked hopefully. 'I was supposed to pick her up at one but apparently she went out and she must have forgotten about the arrangement.'

'Where were you taking her?' Vito was relieved that he was neither insecure nor possessive when it came to women. Growing up with an emotionally unstable father had taught him to despise such behaviour.

'To choose the Christmas tree for the castle from the estate plantation,' his estate manager informed him with a smile. 'And I hoped to fit in lunch.'

Ava was still keeping their affair a big dark secret, Vito registered, and his dark golden eyes smouldered at the realisation. He breathed in slow and deep. 'I'll choose the tree with her tomorrow,' he heard himself declare.

The blond man frowned in surprise but nodded coolly. 'If you see her, tell her I was sorry to miss her.'

Not as sorry as you might have been had you not missed her, Vito reflected with gritted teeth. There were times when Ava infuriated him and this was one of those occasions. Was she attracted to Skeel? Was that why she refused to acknowledge her relationship with Vito? His lovers usually went out of their way to boast about sharing his bed. Given the smallest opportunity they showed him off like a prize and proudly posed by his side for photos. But *not* Ava. Ava attached no strings and imposed strict boundaries. He was, in retrospect, amazed that he had been invited to share her bed. She never, ever asked him what time he would get back home. And she wouldn't phone him, didn't even text. He walked out of the castle in the morning and, for all she knew, he might have been dead five minutes later. But then all that made her one hundred per cent perfect for a guy like him, he reminded himself staunchly. No demands, no avaricious streak, no hidden agenda. What you saw was what you got with Ava and Vito knew how rare a quality that was.

His keen gaze tracked a sudden glimpse of movement on the drive and he registered that it was Ava. On foot and dressed like a bag lady in her jeans and horrible jacket, but even at a distance nothing could outshine her grace of movement or the delicate beauty of her features against her coppery hair. He supposed they were about to have the mother and father of all rows and felt surprisingly insouciant about the fact. He was very focused and persistent when he wanted something, he would wear her down.

'Ava...' Vito greeted her from the wide shallow run of steps at the castle entrance.

Lost in a reverie, Ava glanced up and blinked in surprise. Was it that time already? Surely he shouldn't be home in broad daylight? Like a vampire he was usually only available during the hours of darkness. For a brief moment, she was snatched from her hopeless thoughts by Vito's sheer charismatic appeal. He was truly stunning from his cropped black-as-night hair to his hand-stitched shoes and designer suit. The minute she saw him she wanted to touch him but always quenched the urge, determined not to feed his ego. If he could be cool, she could be even cooler.

Vito threw his big shoulders back and gave her a blinding smile that in a normal mood would have made her suspicious. 'We're going shopping...'

Her lashes fluttered because she didn't know what he was talking about and really couldn't be bothered asking for clarification. Everything felt so far removed from her that a glass wall might as well have separated them.

'And since you're here, let's leave right now,' Vito proposed, descending the steps and closing a hand over hers.

It was second nature to Ava to yank her hand free and say in dismay, 'No—someone might see—'

'It's not like I'm trying to shag you on the front lawn!' Vito flamed back.

'Don't be crude,' Ava told him.

Vito expelled his breath in a furious hiss. He thought of all the years he had spent with *normal* women, greedy, vain, untrustworthy women, who would never have dreamt of pushing him away. And then there was Ava. He stopped dead and closed his arms round her like a prison.

'What you...doing?' she mumbled, all at sea again, an odd distracted air about her.

Vito took advantage. He never failed to take advantage when the right opportunity offered because Ava didn't drop her defences very often. He scooped her up against him so that her feet parted company with the ground and brought his mouth crashing down on hers with devouring eroticism, and that explosion of high-voltage sensation broke through her barriers and she blinked in bewilderment, suddenly depth-charged out of her state of shock. His tongue snaked against hers and a helpless shiver ran through her. He was *so* incredibly sexy, she thought dimly, swept away by the throbbing swelling of her breasts and the hot dart of pulsing warmth between her thighs. He just touched her and she wanted to chain him to the bed. He rocked against her, letting her know that he was equally aroused, and that was when she recalled that they were still in full view of the castle windows and she shimmied down the length of him like a fleeing cat.

'No! I don't want to be seen doing this with you!'

They were already more than halfway to the helicopter. Vito decided not to make an issue of it, although where had not making an issue of Harvey got him? Harvey kept on giving him a paw and nudging him expectantly. Harvey was pushy, desperate to be noticed now that he was sentenced to sleeping downstairs at night, and he stalked Vito round the castle when he was at home. 'He *likes* you,' Ava had said appreciatively but it was not an honour that Vito had sought.

'Where are we going?' Ava prompted suddenly.

'London…shopping,' Vito proffered casually, wondering why she wasn't putting up a fight about the prospect.

'In a helicopter?' Her head ached with the force of the self-discipline she was utilising to hold her flailing emotions in check.

'It'll give us more time.'

'I'm not really in the mood.'

'It's your birthday tomorrow. This is my treat,' Vito pronounced.

Presumably he wanted to buy her a present and if he had organised the trip for her benefit she didn't want to be difficult about it.

'Is there anything wrong? You're very quiet,' Vito commented, leaning down to do up her seat belt for her when she ignored the necessity.

'Thanks.' Ava forced a smile, striving to behave normally. 'No, there's nothing wrong.'

The helicopter rose noisily into the air. Nothing short of physical force would have dragged the truth from Ava about what she had learned from Thomas Fitzgerald earlier that day, she conceded painfully. Apart from the embarrassing reality that the older man still worked for Vito, such a private and wounding revelation had no place in a casual relationship. That was not what she and Vito were about and she would adapt to the sordid discovery that she would never know who her birth father was without anyone's help. But a shopping trip…? Strange, she reflected wearily. She had always assumed that most men didn't like shopping, but at least the pastime would provide a useful distraction from the burden of her unhappy thoughts.

Vito had requested that a personal shopper meet them at Harrods. He cast a questioning glance at Ava as the woman tried to engage her in a discussion about her likes and dislikes but Ava's responses were few and her lack of interest patent. Determined to make the most of the occasion, Vito got involved, chose his favourite colours, nodded and shook his handsome head when outfits were displayed on hangers and freed from the threat of Ava's interference, announced that *everything* was required. With all the animation of a shop window dummy, Ava tried on several garments. That achieved, the outfits began to pile up because Vito shopped as fast as he worked. The personal shopper called in two co-workers to help while Ava continued to hover in an apparent world of her own. Vito stifled his exasperation and decided that unlike most women she had little interest in what she wore. Handbags and shoes joined the pile, along with a beautiful green velvet designer gown, which Vito knew at a glance would be perfect for the party. In the lingerie department, determined to see the back of the gingham pyjamas, he looked to Ava to finally take part in the proceedings because he could not credit that she would let him do the choosing, and he was stunned to see that silent tears were rolling down her cheeks. She seemed totally unaware that she was crying in a public place…

CHAPTER EIGHT

AT Vito's request they were shown into a room with seating and the concerned team assisting them promised to rustle up a cup of tea.

His hands on her slim shoulders, Vito settled Ava down into an armchair as if she were a sleepwalker. He lifted a handful of tissues from a box on the table and pushed them down into her tautly clenched hands. '*Per l'amor di Dio*...what has happened?' he demanded, gazing down at her.

Ava pressed a tissue to her face to dab it dry and wiped her eyes. 'Nothing,' she said gruffly. 'I'm sorry—'

'No, I'm sorry I dragged you out when there's obviously something very wrong. I should have *seen* that you were acting strangely,' he ground out rawly. 'This was supposed to be a treat, not an endurance test that distresses you, *bella mia*—'

Ava stared woodenly down at her knotted hands. 'I'm really sorry...how embarrassing for you to have me behaving like that in public. I'm surprised you didn't walk off and leave me.'

Vito crouched down in front of her and tilted up her chin so that he could better see her reddened blue eyes and the pink tip of her nose. 'Am I that much of a bastard? I will admit to a split second of very masculine panic but that's all.'

Ava encountered beautiful dark golden eyes fever bright with frustration. He hated being out of the loop: she knew that much about him. 'It's not something I can talk about, I'm afraid. I'm all right now, though. The pressure inside me just built up too high and I didn't even realise I was crying.'

'Are you pregnant?' Vito demanded with staggering abruptness.

Ara was taken aback by the question, an involuntary laugh was dredged from her tight throat. Evidently that was *his* biggest fear. 'Of course I'm not and as we've only been together a week, how could I possibly be pregnant?' she whispered just as a knock sounded on the door. 'Or even know that I was?'

'It happens,' Vito said darkly, thinking of Olly, whom his father had sworn had been conceived after a single night. He vaulted upright to open the door and accept the cup of tea that had arrived, settling it down on the table by her side.

'We've been too careful. That's not the problem,' Ava told him dully as she sipped gratefully at the refreshing brew.

'But what *is* the problem?' Vito growled.

'It's nothing to do with you or our relationship and I'm getting over it already,' Ava insisted staunchly, wiping her eyes with determination and blowing her nose, still wincing at the embarrassment of having lost control to such an extent in front of him. 'You see? I'm absolutely fine.'

'You're anything but fine,' Vito contradicted without hesitation. 'You're not yourself at all. Let's finish up and get out of here, but don't think you've heard the last of this. I need to know what's wrong.'

Her face tightened. 'We don't have that kind of relationship.'

'What kind of a relationship do we have?' Vito shot back as she set down the tea and stood up, composed again.

'Fun, casual,' she declared.

Dark colour highlighted his strong cheekbones. 'I can handle problems.'

'You couldn't handle this one and why would you want to anyway?' Ava asked frankly. 'It's not like this is the romance of the century or serious or anything!'

Vito went rigid, his hard jawline clenching, his wide sensual mouth compressing into a surprisingly thin line.

'And now you're offended because I'm not supposed to be that blunt, and maybe you'd just like to say goodbye to me here right this minute!' Ava completed on a rising note of anger.

At that invitation, Vito's eyes flamed burning gold. '*Che cosa hai?* What's the matter with you?'

'I'm giving you an escape route.'

'Shut up,' Vito told her in a seethingly forceful undertone.

Ava drew herself up to her full five feet four inches. 'What did you just say to me?' she demanded.

'Zip it!' Vito bit out with unmistakable savagery. 'Let me tell you what we are going to do. We will complete the shopping trip and leave.'

Ava parted her lips, ready to let loose another volley of the angry aggression that had come out of nowhere to power her mood. Without warning, a rush of screaming anxiety engulfed her next, when she belatedly appreciated that she was actually trying to talk herself out of staying with him for what remained of the week. To her horror, she couldn't accept that prospect, couldn't face the idea of saying goodbye there and then. That acknowledgement shocked her sufficiently into clamping her mouth shut on her dangerously provocative tongue. What the heck was wrong with her? What difference this week or next week? But the threat of separation from Vito managed to flood her with such appalling fear that she couldn't answer her own question.

'I'll take you straight back to the castle when we're finished,' Vito pronounced.

She caught a glimpse of them together in a tall mirror and reddened, thinking that she looked more like a messy teenager than a grown woman in her jeans and jacket. He had to be mortified to be seen out and about with a female that badly dressed and all of a sudden, in spite of the emotions still bubbling inside her like a witch's cauldron, she was ready to make concessions. Her birthday treat? She had thrown his generosity back in his face and wrecked the outing.

Concealing his surprise, Vito watched from a discreet distance as Ava selected lingerie, unwilling to give her an excuse to lose her temper again. What the hell was going on with her? He wondered if he would ever understand her, wondered why he should even want to when he was usually up and out at the first sign of complications in an affair. But she had never been moody with him before. She vanished into a changing room with a bundle of garments.

Ava stripped, glanced in dismay at a couple of tags marked with eye-watering prices and wondered if he was insane to be spending so much money on her when they only had another week together. But it could be a good week just like the first if she could only stop thinking about the ending that would come with it. Her mouth down curved at the lowering thought that she was certainly in the mood to please as she put on a dress: *he* liked dresses, dropped hints like bricks around her about feminine clothes, loved her legs. And her bottom and her breasts. Just not *her*! Her eyes prickled. She couldn't even blame him. His brother was dead because of what she had done. What she had now with Vito was the most she could ever have because he would never be able to surmount that barrier between them.

Vito's was not the only male head to turn in the vicinity when Ava reappeared, a slim chic beauty in a form-fitting dress, jacket and high heels.

'Am I allowed to jump you in the limo?' Vito growled, hot golden eyes pinned to her face.

Ava laughed. She knew she looked good, hadn't frankly known she could look that good in a new outfit and was very aware that she had him and the helpful saleswomen to thank for it because she had virtually no experience of either choosing or wearing more decorative formal clothes.

'No,' she told him, suppressing the memories of Thomas Fitzgerald, her late mother and her wretched childhood. She would get over it, adapt to the new knowledge about herself, much as she had adapted to other things.

Having emerged from the shop, a procession of bags and boxes already piled into the limousine awaiting them, Vito closed an arm round her spine. Suddenly a man called out Vito's name and he halted in surprise. A blinding flash lit them up and a man with a camera shot them a cheeky smile before taking off into the depths of the milling crowds on the pavement.

'My word, why did he want to take a picture of us?' Ava asked as Vito tucked her into the car.

'He's probably paparazzi.' But the incident sent a vague sense of unease filtering through Vito because he was not accustomed to that kind of press intrusion in his life. 'I can't imagine why he wanted a photo of us.'

'He knew your name. You must get a lot of that sort of attention,' Ava assumed.

'Usually only in the business papers and if I have a celebrity on my arm, which is rare these days,' Vito confided, a frown drawing his fine ebony brows together. 'I'm a very private person. I don't know what the source of his interest might have been.'

'I hardly think it was me.'

'You do look stunning,' Vito countered reflectively.

Self-conscious colour lit her fair complexion. In her fancy feathers, she felt ridiculously vulnerable. 'Where are we going now?'

'You look stunning. I shall keep on saying it until you acknowledge it, *bella mia.*'

Ava ignored him. She had earned very few compliments in her life and never knew how to handle them. Deep down inside she thought he only said such things because he believed all women expected it and she despised insincerity.

'I originally planned for us to spend the night in my city apartment.'

'Didn't know you had one.'

'It's handy when I'm flying in late from abroad or working through the night. But you're not in the mood for dining and clubbing, are you?' Vito murmured lazily.

'I'm in full party-pooper mode,' Ava admitted with a grimace. 'Sorry. I'd just like to go—'

'Home,' Vito slotted in. 'When situations change, I adapt quickly.'

Her fingernails curled in silent protest into the wool jacket on her lap. His home, not hers. The locality had nothing to offer her now. She no longer had a home base. So what had changed? she asked herself irritably, angry that she still felt so bruised and alone. The people she had believed were her family until earlier that day had long since made it clear that they wanted nothing to do with her anyway, consequently it was over-sensitive to still be feeling so gutted about it. Suck it up, she told herself irritably.

Studying the tension etched in her delicate profile, Vito wanted to shake Ava like a money box the way you do to extract the last stubborn coin. What was wrong with the rational approach of telling him what the problem was so that he could sort it out? That would settle things and she would return to normal and stop being so polite and silent. Maybe he should have let her dump him. He had never been dumped. Was that why he was still with her even though she was being an absolute pain? She was screwing with his head. He knew she was doing it but had yet to work out how.

Dusk was falling by the time Ava mounted the steps to the entrance of Bolderwood Castle. She walked in the big front door and was instantly enfolded in a ridiculously soothing sense of security. A log fire was crackling in the huge hall grate, flickering warm inviting shadows over the ornamented garlands and the tall ivy-draped glass candle vases on the mantelpiece. It looked beautiful and painfully familiar at one and the same time. She could remember roasting chestnuts by the fire with Olly, laughing when he sang a Christmas song off-key. While she was thinking, Harvey hurtled past her and bounced up to greet Vito first with fawning enthusiasm. Ava looked on without comment, having already accepted that Harvey was, at heart it seemed, a man's dog, for as soon as Vito had become a regular fixture in Harvey's life Harvey had firmly attached himself to him.

'Don't put hair on me,' Vito warned the dog, patting his head to make him go away again, but Harvey was a needy dog and he kept on pushing for more.

'He doesn't shed hair—we think it's the poodle in him.'

'Poodle?' Vito repeated in disbelief, surveying Harvey, who was a large animal by any standards and very disreputable in appearance with his floppy ears and messy curly coat. 'Aren't poodles little and fluffy?'

'There are big ones too but…Harvey is a mongrel.'

Harvey looked up at Vito with round brown pleading eyes and nudged his thigh again. Vito sighed heavily. 'All right. He can stay.'

Shaken, Ava stared up at him. 'For good…*here?* Are you serious?'

'I wouldn't have said it if I wasn't,' Vito imparted wryly.

Ava gave a yelp of delight, hurled herself at Vito and locked her arms round his neck in a display of natural exuberance. 'You won't regret it, Vito. He's very loyal and loving and he'll protect you if anyone ever threatens you.'

Vito stared down at the animated triangle of her face, transfixed by the complete transformation that had taken place. 'Nobody has ever threatened me.'

'He'll want to sleep beside your bed.'

'That's an undesirable trait, Ava.' But he locked his arms round her slim supple body and drew her up to his level to extract a passionate kiss, noting that her bright blue eyes were almost laughably disconcerted by his sudden unexpected assault. 'Of course you can sleep beside my bed any time you like...but I'd prefer you *in* it, *gioia mia*.'

In that instant being wanted felt unbelievably wonderful to Ava's battered emotions and in response her own hunger consumed her in a great greedy flood. As Vito toyed with her soft full lower lip, teasing, stroking the delicate interior, she angled her head back, shamelessly inviting more. With an appreciative growl, he curved his strong hands round her bottom and hoisted her up against him, making her violently aware of the fullness of his erection.

'Bed...*now*,' Vito husked against her lush mouth as he carried her upstairs. 'I can't wait...'

And secure in his arms, Ava wondered when the attraction between them had become so powerful that her body simply reacted without her awareness, the peaks of her breasts straining full and tight with arousal, the secret place at the heart of her intensely hot. She could no longer control the desperate urgency and need eating her alive from inside out. He set her down on the bed, where she peeled off her jacket, kicked off her high heels and shimmied out of her dress like a shameless hussy eager to meet her fate. He stood in front of her, stripping, and he didn't stop until he was naked, a lithe bronzed vision of muscular male perfection, uninhibited in his urgent arousal. He leant over her, crushing and tasting her luscious mouth, his tongue dallying, delving deep to ramp up her yearning. And throughout that exercise he was undressing her with deft hands, peeling away her new and delicate floral underwear. Long fingers playing with the protruding pink buds of her breasts, he made her gasp and part her slender thighs, hips digging into the mattress beneath her.

'You're so sexy,' he groaned against her swollen mouth when he lifted her up against him, the long thick column of his erection hot against her stomach. 'I've never wanted a woman like this...I'm burning up.'

He brought her down on her knees on the bed in front of him, reaching down to stimulate the tiny, unbearably sensitive nub at her core. An almost anguished whimper of sound was wrenched from her tight throat. Her breath was coming in shallow pants, her whole body poised on the edge of an anticipation so intense it hurt. He stroked her and she flinched, aching and hypersensitive to the caress.

'You're so ready for me, *bella mia.* That really fires me up,' Vito growled in her ear as he nudged her thighs further apart, his hands running up and down her slender spine and dropping lower to touch the swollen buds of her breasts.

'Please...' she moaned, wild with impatience, twisting her head round, catching a glimpse of the smouldering dark golden eyes fixed to her.

His hands firm on her hips Vito thrust into her hard and deep and groaned with earthy satisfaction. Her inner muscles gripped him as a shockwave of amazing sensation engulfed her. She threw back her head and moaned. As he sank into her raw excitement made her heartbeat race. She quivered, insanely receptive to his dominance, and then sobbed as the melting waves of delirious pleasure engulfing her swept her up higher and higher until she reached the ultimate peak. While Vito thrust into her with a final forceful twist of his hips and a savage shout of release, Ava was shattered by the power of her own climax. An ecstatic cry tore from her lips and she slid forward onto her stomach, all strength drained from her satiated limbs.

'Your passion is the perfect match for mine,' Vito breathed with satisfaction, kissing the nape of her neck with lingering appreciation and slowly pulling back to release her from his weight. Just as suddenly he fell still again.

Recognising the change in the atmosphere, Ava turned over to stare up into his stunned dark eyes. 'What?' she pressed with a frown.

In answer, Vito used his strong hands to turn her back over onto her stomach again. 'You finally took the plaster off...I had no idea it was hiding a tattoo.' A wondering forefinger traced the pattern of the ink marking on her left hip. It was a heart pierced by an arrow with a name in the centre. *His* name.

Aghast at the news that she had lost the plaster, guessing it must have come off in the shower that morning, Ava turned over again so fast that she was breathless. 'You *saw* it?' she gasped strickenly, swift hot colour washing up beneath her fair skin as extreme mortification gripped her.

Vito nodded slowly, thoughtfully. 'As a rule I'm not into tattoos but I think I can live with you having my name branded on one hip,' he breathed tautly, wicked amusement fighting to pull at the corners of his firmly controlled mouth. 'When did you get that done?'

Her face still burning with the intensity of her embarrassment, Ava sat up, hugging her knees defensively, her eyes shielded by her lashes. 'I was eighteen on a girlie holiday in Spain. It was a drunken dare and I went for it because some of the other girls were getting stuff done and it seemed like a good idea at the time...but it was very stupid.'

'Eighteen?' Vito grimaced. 'No, it wasn't a good idea to have a name put on your body at that age.'

'I've regretted it ever since.'

Vito closed his arms round her small tense figure, a wolfish smile suddenly slashing his handsome mouth. 'I like it. It appeals to something primitive in me, *bella mia*.'

'I'll probably save up and get it removed some day,' Ava muttered, ignoring his comment.

'You were so young in those days,' Vito remarked ruefully.

'But I'm all grown up now,' Ava reminded him, keen to drop the subject, that place on her hip still burning as though she had been touched by a naked flame. As she turned to glance at the clock by the bed she froze and exclaimed, 'Oh, no, I was supposed to meet Damien at lunchtime and I totally forgot about him!'

'I'll take you to choose a tree tomorrow.'

Ava's mouth fell wide in shock. '*You*...will?'

A fine ebony brow elevated. 'Why not me?'

'Crashing about in the undergrowth looking at trees isn't really your thing,' Ava challenged.

Never having been a fan of the great outdoors, Vito

didn't argue with that assessment. He stretched out beside her in the tumbled sheets and folded her to him with determined hands. 'I have no choice. Damien's trying too hard to get with you.'

Her bright blue eyes sparkled with amusement. 'I can handle Damien. You can be very possessive.'

'I'm not the possessive type. Easy come, easy go, that's me,' Vito told her with unassailable assurance and then he frowned, his black brows pleating as he suddenly sat up again to stare down at her in consternation. 'I didn't use a condom!'

Ava winced, unable to hide her dismay or her surprise that he could have been so careless. 'I wasn't thinking either,' she sighed in grudging acknowledgement of their mutual passion, already engaged in mentally working out where she was in her cycle. 'We should be all right, though. It was the wrong time.'

'*Any* time can be dangerous when it comes to conception,' Vito countered, his face taut with disquiet. '*Accidenti!* I was so excited I forgot—that's never happened to me before.'

'There's always a first time. I think we'll get away with it,' Ava reassured.

Too shaken by his oversight, Vito said nothing. He could not believe that even in the heat of passion he had overlooked the need for precautions. He had never made that mistake before. There was something about Ava that destroyed his usual innate caution. Unlike her, however, he wasn't an eternal optimist and he was already thinking, What if she's pregnant? If it happened, he would deal with it. After all, he was not a panic-stricken teenaged boy.

* * *

The next morning, Ava looked in growing wonderment at the vast collection of clothes that filled the boxes, garment bags and carriers in one corner of her bedroom. What on earth had come over Vito? She was only with him another week and he had bought her more clothes than she could wear out in several years of sustained use! While she stowed away the garments she selected a pair of jeans, woollen sweater and a quilted jacket to wear and quickly got dressed to go down for breakfast.

'Happy birthday,' Vito declared from his stance by the fireplace, where a crackling fire took the chill from the room. 'Are you sure you want to choose the tree today? It's exceptionally cold.'

'The party schedule is tight. It has to be today so that I can dress the tree tomorrow.' Ava tried very hard not to stare at him. After all, it was barely forty minutes since they had parted in her room to shower and dress. Now, just like her, Vito was casually clad, a powerfully masculine figure who dominated the room with his presence. The strong hard bones of his face allied to the deep-set brilliance of his spectacular dark eyes gave him a sizzling charismatic appeal that ignited every cell in her body. He lit her fire, he floated her boat, he turned her on, she acknowledged abstractedly, instinctively struggling to fight free of the sexual charge he put out, wishing she were less of a pushover in that category. She badly needed distance, rational thought and a cool head…but terrifyingly none of those necessities were at her disposal.

Vito tugged out a chair by the table for her in an effortless display of courtesy that made her tense. He treated her as though she required his care and protection and, although his attitude often jarred with her staunchly independent spirit, she was also aware that on some level he was satisfying a secret craving deep down inside her. 'We're having pancakes this morning—my housekeeper tells me they're your favourite,' he announced.

A wash of over-emotional tears momentarily stung Ava's eyes. Nobody had ever made a fuss about her birthday before. Indeed on several occasions that special date had been entirely overlooked. Equipped as she now was with the true facts of her background, Ava could understand why her mother had sometimes found it easier to simply ignore her youngest daughter's birthday. In many ways, Ava conceded ruefully, she had been a neglected child, who was neither properly fed nor clothed, while her teenaged sisters had often stayed at friends' houses to avoid coming home, leaving Ava alone with her alcoholic and often insensible mother.

Wary of the surge of her unstable emotions and distressing memories, Ava tucked into the pancakes with determined appetite. A small, square jewellery box sat beside her plate and she rigorously ignored it, scared of what it might contain. My goodness, hadn't he spent enough money on her during the shopping trip? What else might he have given her?

'Aren't you going to open it?' Vito finally prompted.

'It embarrasses me when you spend money on me.'

'It didn't cost me anything.'

Intrigued, Ava reached for it and opened it. Her heart jolted to a sudden halt and she swallowed with difficulty because the box contained Olly's gold St Christopher medal. 'You can't give me this.'

In answer, Vito sprang upright, hooked the chain onto his fingers and nudged her hair out of the way to place it round her neck. 'You should have something to remember him by, *cara mia*,' he said flatly.

'Thank you…' Ava said shakily as the cool metal settled against her skin. She was painfully touched by the gift. It could surely only mean that Vito had moved beyond thinking of her solely as his brother's killer to recall instead her once close and loving friendship with his sibling. For that piece of undeserved good fortune she was eternally grateful.

'It once belonged to my father and Olly cherished it. Come on,' Vito urged hurriedly as her mouth trembled. 'It's time to pick the tree…'

Ava hastily swallowed back the thickness of tears clogging her vocal cords and clattered down the steps in his wake with Harvey to climb into the waiting four-wheel drive. Vito drove down rutted tracks to the coni-fer plantation at the back of the estate and vaulted out to retrieve a paint tin and brush with which to mark the chosen tree. The icy breeze stung her damp cheeks. Her hand stole up to brush the St Christopher at her throat. St Christopher, the patron saint of safe journeys. Olly hadn't been wearing it the night of the crash because the chain had broken.

She trudged into the great stand of trees, banish-ing recollections of long-gone Christmases with rig-orous self-discipline. In the mood she was in the last thing she needed to be doing was wallowing in the past, she conceded humbly. She paused in front of a fifteen-foot-tall conifer with a model shape and dense branches that skirted it almost to the ground. 'That's definitely the one.'

Vito marked it with the paint and set down the tin to ram his chilled hands into the pockets of his jacket, standing tall and braced into the wind clawing his black hair back from his darkly handsome features. 'That was quick.'

'It's a classic...oh my goodness, it's snowing!' Ava carolled, hurrying into the clearing open to the sky to raise her hands to the fat white flakes floating slowly down.

Vito watched her chase snowflakes, her bright blue eyes intent against her breeze-stung complexion, her vibrant copper hair anchored below a cream woollen hat. She had no thought of what she might look like, no concern that he might laugh at her. She was as un-inhibited in her enjoyment as a child, her enchantment etched in her face with an innocence she had yet to lose. Seeing that vulnerability disturbed him, put him in mind of the fact that even her family had rejected her. It was the belated acknowledgement that her family lived only down the road that prompted him to say, 'I think it's time you visited your family.'

Ava froze. 'Been there, done that,' she declared stiffly without looking at him as she stooped to lift up the paint tin. 'I'm freezing...let's get back to the car—'

'When did you visit them?'

'Yesterday,' she extended reluctantly.

Vito frowned and made the connection, shrewd dark eyes bronzing with sudden intensity. 'What the hell happened?'

'I found out that I'm not Thomas Fitzgerald's daughter, after all. I'm a bastard, father unknown,' she confided doggedly between gritted teeth as she stalked ahead of him towards the car.

'You're...a *what*?' Vito closed a strong hand round

her slim shoulder to force her to turn her head to look
back at him again.

Ava explained what she had learned in as few words
as she could manage. 'So, you see, you really couldn't
expect any of them to have visited me while I was in
prison or to bother with me now—I'm not and never
have been part of their family and they finally feel that
they can be open about that.'

Appalled, Vito swore under his breath in Italian.
'You should have been told a long time ago and never
in such a cruel manner.'

'Nobody was cruel!' Ava interrupted in heated dis-
agreement. 'Thomas Fitzgerald was fed up with having
to live a lie and you can't blame him for that.'

'I—'

Her eyes flashed with anger. 'It's none of your
blasted business!'

Silenced by that forthright declaration, Vito drove
back to the castle with a fiercely tense atmosphere between them. Ava breathed in slow and deep, fighting
to control her distress. She hadn't wanted to tell him
but he had virtually forced her to speak. Now he had
to be embarrassed for her but the last thing she wanted
or needed was his pity. Every atom of her being reared
up in a rage at that humiliating prospect.

Eleanor Dobbs was waiting for them in the big hall.
The housekeeper's expression was grave and anxiety
infiltrated Ava as the older woman extended a folded
newspaper to her employer.

Vito glanced at the headline, *'Barbieri with bro's
slayer,'* and the accompanying photographs, one of Ava
at the time of the accident, the other of her by his side
in London the day before. His handsome mouth com-

pressed into a tough line while Ava peered over his arm to study the same article and turned white as the snow beginning to lie on the ground outside.

CHAPTER NINE

PRESSED into the library, Ava filched the newspaper from Vito to get a proper look at the article. She spread it out on his desk and poured over it to read every word while he remained poised by the fire to defrost, his expression forbidding and stormy.

'This is horrible,' she muttered in disgust.

'It is what it is,' Vito responded stonily. 'The truth we can't change. I can't sue anyone for telling the truth but I wish I'd chosen to be more discreet in your company yesterday. What I *do* want to know is where they got the tip-off from. I will be questioning my staff. Nobody else knew you were here.'

The truth we can't change. That statement rang like the crack of doom in Ava's ears and her heart sank to the soles of her feet. It *was* the truth, the elephant in the room whenever they were together. Serving a prison sentence hadn't cleared her name, rehabilitated her reputation or made her one less jot guilty as charged of reckless endangerment of Olly's life. She stilled on that thought, cold inside and outside, her skin turning clammy. Maybe this was the real punishment for what she had done, she conceded, never ever being able to forget for longer than a moment in time.

Vito strode to the door. 'I'll talk to the staff.'

'Wait…at least one other person knew I was here,' Ava volunteered abruptly. 'I was visiting Olly's grave and she recognised me. I thought I'd seen her before somewhere but I didn't *know* her—Katrina Orpington?'

Halfway out of the door, Vito came to a sudden halt. 'Katrina? The vicar's stepdaughter?'

'Is she? Blonde? Looks a bit like a model? She called me a killer, thought it was offensive that I should be in the cemetery,' Ava advanced woodenly.

Vito's gaze flared hot gold. 'And you didn't warn me? *Dio mio,* is there anything you're willing to tell me?'

Her troubled eyes veiled and her soft lips firmed. 'You don't need to hear that kind of stuff.'

'I don't need to be shielded from it either!' Vito growled, his anger unhidden.

In the simmering silence Ava perused the newspaper again. No, on one score Vito had proved correct: the item contained no lies, simply the facts inviting people to make their own judgement of how appropriate it was for Vito to be entertaining his brother's killer. In the photo taken yesterday, having taken fright at the sudden appearance of the photographer, she was clinging to Vito, leaving little room for doubt that theirs was an intimate relationship. The article would certainly raise brows and rouse condemnation. Her face burned, guilt and regret assailing her. Vito had been good to her. He did not deserve public embarrassment on her behalf. She should never have come to Bolderwood: returning to the scene of her crime had been asking for trouble. It hurt that she had made the mistake but that Vito was being asked to pay the price.

All she could do was leave: the solution was that

simple. Gossiping tongues would fall silent once people realised she was no longer around. She hurried upstairs to her room, dug her rucksack out from between
the wardrobe and the wall and proceeded to pack it with
her original collection of sparse clothing. She discarded
the outfit he had bought her but kept on the underwear.
She wondered if someone would give her a lift to the
local railway station, checked her purse to see if she had
enough for the fare: she *didn't*. She would ask Vito for a
sub on her salary although she cringed at the prospect
of directly approaching him for money and accepting
it from him. It would feel downright sleazy.

Without warning the door opened. Vito scanned the
small pile of clothing on the bed, the open rucksack,
and shot a gleaming, cutting look at her that would have
withered a weaker woman. '*Madre di Dio!* What the
hell are you doing?'

Ava ducked the direct question. 'I should never have
come here in the first place—it was asking for trouble!
I did try to warn you about that.'

Vito shifted a silencing hand. 'Enough with the lie-
down-and-die mentality,' he derided. 'You're tougher
than that.'

'Maybe I thought I was but I've just realised that
you can't beat social expectations, you can't flout the
system and then complain when you become a target.'

'No, you can't if you're a coward.'

Blue eyes darkening with fury, Ava pushed her chin
up. 'I'm not a coward.'

'You're getting ready to scuttle out of here like a rat
leaving a sinking ship,' Vito contradicted without hesitation. 'What else is that but cowardice?'

'I'm not a coward!' Ava proclaimed, inflamed by the charge. 'I can take the heat.'

'Then take it and stay.'

Ava snatched in an uneasy breath. 'It's not that simple. You don't need this…er…trouble right now.'

Vito squared his big broad shoulders. 'I thrive on trouble.'

Ava tore her strained gaze from the bold challenge in his features, her heartbeat quickening. She wondered how long it would be before she could picture that darkly beautiful face without that happening. Here she was, twenty-two years old, and she was as infatuated as a teenager with a man who could only hurt her. That was not a record to boast about and the best thing she could do for both of them was sever the connection in a quick, clean cut that would cause the least possible damage. Vito was a stubborn guy. The very idea that he should conform to social mores was anathema to him. Vito was always ready to fight to the death to defend his own right to do as he liked. A textbook knee-jerk reaction from an arrogant, aggressive male.

'Look,' Ava breathed on a more measured note, 'all the party arrangements are in place. I'll leave clear notes and contact details for all the outside help I engaged—'

'I don't give a flying…*damn*…' he selected between gritted white teeth '…about the party! You know how I feel about Christmas.'

'Can Harvey still stay?' Ava prompted anxiously.

The animal concerned voiced a little whine and pushed his muzzle anxiously against Vito's thigh, his need for reassurance in the tense atmosphere pronounced.

Vito groaned out loud at the question. 'I think you'd have to kidnap him to take him away.'

Ava nodded woodenly because she knew she was going to miss Harvey's easy companionship and affection. Of course she would miss Vito too but that would be *good* for her, character-building, she told herself urgently. She had let herself get too dependent on Vito and that was dangerous. It was better to get out now on her terms at a time of her choosing rather than wait for his inevitable rejection. 'I have to leave.'

'You're not going anywhere,' Vito decreed harshly.

'Be reasonable,' Ava urged. 'I can't stay after that story was published in the papers…as if people around here even need reminding of what I did!'

'It doesn't bother me,' Vito fired back without scruple.

'Well, it bothers me!' Ava flared back at him out of all patience, her hands planted on her slim hips for emphasis. 'And what difference does it make anyway? So, we part a few days earlier? This was only ever going to last two weeks.'

Eyes smouldering between thick black lashes over that assessment, Vito shifted closer with silent fluid grace. 'Says who?'

'Says me!' Ava thumped her chest in emphasis with a loosely coiled fist. 'Do you think I'm stupid, Vito? Did you think I wouldn't appreciate that once the party was over, we were too?'

His face set even harder. 'I never said that.'

'Yeah, like you were planning to come calling at my humble bedsit on a regular basis!' Ava scoffed in disbelief. 'Why can't you at least be honest about what we have here?'

'Do you think that could be because when I dare to disagree with you, you immediately accuse me of subterfuge?' Vito queried smooth as silk, a sardonic ebony brow raised.

Ava was getting more and more worked up over her inability to get through to him. He was dancing around words, refusing to match her candour, selfishly complicating things when she wanted it all done and dusted, neat and tidy and over while she still had the strength to deal with it. Before she even realised what she was doing, both her hands lifted in frustration and thumped his broad hard chest instead. 'It's *over,* Vito! Fun while it lasted but now the writing's on the wall.'

'Not on my wall,' Vito fielded, closing strong hands round her waist and lifting her right off her startled feet to lay her down on the well-sprung bed.

'What the heck are you talking about?' Ava snapped back at him in bewilderment, scrambling breathlessly back against the headboard to stay out of his reach.

'*My* agenda, rather than yours…sorry about that,' Vito delivered rawly, dark golden eyes glittering like starlight in his lean taut features as he came down on his knees at the foot of the big bed and began to move closer again. 'It's not over for me yet. Sorry, if that disrupts your rigid timetable. But I still want you…'

Sentenced to involuntary stillness by his extraordinary behaviour, Ava stared fixedly at him. He was stalking her like a predatory jungle cat ready to pounce. 'Now just you stop right there!' she warned him shrilly.

She drove him insane, Vito acknowledged darkly. Somehow every time they clashed she brought emotion into it, the emotion he shunned and she unleashed like a tidal wave. 'I'm not stopping,' Vito almost purred with assurance. 'And you know I don't back down...'

That dark sensual voice of his was compelling, sending a deeply responsive echo strumming right through her taut length. 'You know I'm right, Vito.'

'You always think you're right,' Vito husked. 'But on this occasion, you're wrong. I want you.'

A jolt of desire shot through her, making her achingly aware of the heat at her feminine core. Her cheeks burned with mortification. 'We only got out of bed a couple of hours ago!' she slung.

'And I'm still hungry, *bella mia,*' Vito growled deep in his chest, drawing level with her to bend his head. 'Doesn't that disprove your theory that I'm ready to let you go?'

'You don't *let* me do anything!' Ava launched back at him in a rage. 'And I know you well enough to know that you won't be ready to let me go until *you* make that decision.'

His fingers feathered slowly through her tousled coppery hair and curved to her taut jaw. 'You're a lot of hard work but I still burn for you.'

Ava flung back her head in defiance. 'Well, my flame's gone out. Common sense snuffed it,' she traded.

'What the hell does common sense have to do with this?' Vito demanded thickly, crushing her stubbornly compressed mouth beneath his and revelling in the way her soft full lips opened for him as the tip of his tongue scored that sealed seam.

His mouth devoured her and she wanted to eat him alive, powered by a frantic desire that terrified her when she was trying so hard to make him see sense. But there was no sense in that all-encompassing overwhelming hunger that gripped her. Her hands came up of their own volition to cup his high cheekbones and then threaded into his thick silky hair. The spicy scent and taste of him only made her want more...*always* more. When did she reach satiation level? When would that terrible craving ease enough to allow her to hold it at bay?

'I'm packed, I'm leaving,' she mumbled obstinately when he freed her swollen mouth long enough to let her breathe again.

'I could chain you to the headboard to keep you here,' Vito told her silkily as he closed a possessive hand round a full breast below her sweater, a thumb massaging the already swollen peak. 'Now doesn't that open an interesting field of possibilities?'

Ava trembled, sexual frissons of sensation running through her like liquid lightning. 'Only if you're a perv,' she told him doggedly.

'You like it when I'm dominant in bed,' Vito traded with fiery erotic assurance in his stunning eyes.

Ava planted her hands to his shoulders and pushed forward, off balancing him back against the pillows. A wolfish grin split his bronzed features and he laughed with rich appreciation, hauling her down on top of him with shocking strength to take her mouth again with ravishing force. She shivered violently, insanely aware of the male arousal resting like a red-hot brand against her and the hand sliding down over her quivering stomach below her unfastened jeans to tease her with knowing expertise.

'Don't forget that I'm an equal opportunities employer,' Vito reminded her raggedly, lifting her out of her jeans with more haste than finesse.

'I'm in the middle of packing!' Ava raked at him in

a frustration steadily becoming more laced with self-loathing.

'But you're not going anywhere now,' Vito pointed out, shedding his jeans with positive violence and drawing her back up against him, all hot and ready and hard.

'We should have discussed this like civilised adults—'

'You talk too much,' Vito told her, delicately tracing her lush opening with carnal skill and then, having established her readiness from the whimper of anguished sound that exited her straining lungs, he shifted over her and sank into her with a raw primal sound of satisfaction that she found insanely arousing.

That fast the moment to stand her ground was lost and her body took over, her hips angling up to accept more of him…and then more and then, heavens, the pulsing, driving fullness of him was pushing her closer and closer to the edge she had never thought to visit again with him.

In the aftermath, his heart still thundering over hers, she held him close, adoring the weight and intimacy of him that close, wanting and barely resisting the urge to cover him in kisses. But while her body was satisfied, her brain was not and with every minute that passed she was seeing deeper into herself. She wanted to run away because she was scared of getting hurt. Why was she likely to get hurt? Solely because she felt too much for him. She was hopelessly, deeply and irretrievably attached to Vito Barbieri, indeed as much in love as a woman could be with a man. For too long she had denied her true feelings, suppressed them and refused out of fear to examine them.

'And now you're thinking too much…for a sensible adult,' Vito reproved, noting her evasively lowered lashes and mutinously closed lips before he lowered his handsome head to rub a stubbled cheek against the soft slope of her breast and drink in the familiar scent of her with a sense of bone-deep satisfaction. 'This isn't complex. We're in a good place right now...don't spoil it, *gioia mia*.'

'I need a shower,' she said stubbornly, whipping her clinging arms off him again.

'You are *so* obstinate,' Vito grated, rolling off her with sudden alacrity and viewing her with forbidding cool from the other side of the bed.

'Whatever turns you on,' Ava replied glibly.

And she did, any time of day, every time, *all* the time, Vito mused grudgingly, watching the lithe swing of her slim curvy hips and spotting the tattoo of his name inked onto her pale skin as she vanished into the bathroom. Ava had taught him what a weekend was, how to walk away from work, daydream in important meetings. She was like an express train to a side of life he had never known before and sometimes it spooked him. He should have let her leave, a little voice intoned deep in the back of his mind, get his work focus back on track, return to...*normal*? Yet being with Ava felt astonishingly normal even when her backchat was ricocheting off the walls around him. The phone by the bed buzzed and he flipped over to answer it.

In the shower, Ava was scrubbing the wanton evidence of her weakness from her skin when Vito appeared in the doorway, a towering bronzed figure with a physique to die for.

She rammed the shower door back. 'Don't I get peace anywhere?' she sniped.

'That was Eleanor on the phone. Your sisters have arrived for a visit—she put them in the drawing room.'

Ava froze in stark shock and equally sudden pleasure. 'Gina and Bella have come here to see me?'

'Obviously they read that newspaper article...or your ex-father figure talked. Dress up,' Vito advised. 'You don't want them feeling sorry for you.'

'Or thinking that you would consort with a poorly dressed woman,' Ava completed cheekily.

'I'd consort with you no matter what you wore,' Vito imparted with a lazy sardonic smile.

'But you probably prefer me in nothing,' Ava pointed out drily.

Her mind awash with speculation, Ava dug in haste through her extensive collection of new clothes. Gina and Bella, both in their thirties, were always well groomed. Vito's comment had struck a raw nerve. Ava didn't want to look like an object of pity, particularly after the humble letters she had sent in hope of renewed contact with her siblings had been ignored. So, why on earth were they coming to see her now? Her generous mouth down curved as she wondered if her sisters were planning to ask her to leave the neighbourhood to protect them from embarrassment. Gina, married to an engineer, and Bella, married to a solicitor, had always seemed very conscious of what their friends and neighbours might think of their mother and her drink problems. Elegant in a soft dove-grey dress teamed with a pale lavender cardigan, her revealingly tumbled hair carefully secured to the back of her head, Ava slid her feet into heels and went downstairs.

Nerves were eating her alive by the time she opened the drawing-room door. Vito was not there. Gina and

Bella were small, blonde and curvy like their late mother and both women swiftly stood up to look at her. Recognising the pronounced lack of physical similarity between her sisters and herself, Ava marvelled that it had not previously occurred to her to wonder if they had had different parentage.

'I hope you don't mind us calling in for a chat,' Gina said awkwardly. 'We came on impulse after seeing that photo of you in the paper with Vito Barbieri. Dad didn't realise that you were staying here at the castle when you visited him and Janet yesterday.'

'I don't think he would have cared had I come down on a rocket from the moon,' Ava declared wryly as she sat down opposite the other two women. 'I was only in their home for about five minutes and once he'd said his piece there didn't seem to be anything more to say.'

'Well, actually there is more,' Bella spoke up tensely. 'Dad might still feel that he has an axe to grind over the fact that he chose to pretend that you were his child all those years but, no matter what Mum did, you're *still* our sister, Ava.'

'Half-sister,' Ava qualified stiffly, unable to forget her unanswered letters. 'And let's face it, we've never been close.'

'We may have grown up in a very dysfunctional family,' Gina acknowledged, compressing her lips. 'But we don't agree with the way Dad is behaving now. He's made everything more difficult for the three of us. He demanded that we keep you out of our lives. He prefers to act like you don't exist.'

'And for too long we played along with Dad for the sake of family peace,' Bella admitted unhappily.

'And sometimes we used his attitude to you as an

excuse as well,' Gina added guiltily. 'Like us not coming to see you while you were in prison. To be frank, I didn't *want* to go into a prison and be vetted and then searched like a criminal just for the privilege of visiting you.'

'We did once get as close as the prison gates,' Bella volunteered with a wince of embarrassed uneasiness.

'*Prison*-visiting…it just seemed so sordid,' Gina confided more frankly. 'And the gates and the guards were intimidating.'

'I can understand that,' Ava said and she did.

Eleanor Dobbs entered with a laden tray of coffee and cakes, providing a welcome distraction from the tension stretching between the three women.

'Mum wrote a letter to you just before she died,' Gina volunteered once the door had closed behind the housekeeper again.

Ava sat up straight and almost spilt her cup of coffee in the process. 'A…*letter*?'

'That's *why* we tried to work ourselves up to come and visit you—to give you the letter,' Bella confessed.

'Why didn't you just post it to me?' Ava demanded angrily. 'Why didn't anyone ask if I could visit her before she died? I didn't even know she was ill.'

'Mum passed away very quickly,' Gina told the younger woman heavily. 'Her liver was wrecked. Dad didn't want you informed and Mum insisted that she couldn't face seeing you again, so we couldn't see the point of telling you that she was dying.'

Ava absorbed those wounding facts without comment. News of her mother's death had come as a shocking bolt from the blue while she was in prison. She had been excluded from the entire process. Now she had to accept the even harsher truth that, even dying, her mother had rejected a chance for a last meeting with her. 'The letter...' she began again tightly.

Bella grimaced. 'We didn't post it because we know prisons go over everything offenders get in the post and the idea of that happening to Mum's last words didn't feel right. But we've brought it with us...not that it's likely to be of much comfort to you.'

'Towards the end Mum's mind was wandering. The letter's more of a note and it makes no sense.' Gina withdrew an envelope from her handsome leather bag and passed it across the coffee table.

'So, you've read it, then,' Ava gathered.

'I had to write it for her, Ava. She was too weak to hold a pen,' Bella explained uncomfortably. 'It's obvious that she was feeling very guilty about you and she did want you to know that.'

Ava's hand trembled and tightened its grip on the crumpled envelope. She still felt that her sisters could have made more of an effort to ensure that the letter came to her sooner but she said nothing.

'We all loved her but she wasn't a normal mum,' Gina remarked awkwardly. 'Or even a decent wife and we all suffered for that.'

Her attention resting on Ava's pinched profile, Bella grimaced and murmured, 'Let's leave this subject alone for the moment. Are we allowed to satisfy our crazy curiosity and ask what you're doing living in Bolderwood Castle?'

'I'm organising the Christmas party for Vito,' Ava advanced. 'Everything else just sort of happened.'

'Everything else?' Gina probed delicately. 'You used to be besotted with him.'

'I got over that,' Ava declared, privately reflecting that proximity to Vito and a closer understanding with him had merely made her reach a whole new level of besottedness.

'Come on, Ava. The whole countryside is talking and you're killing us here,' Bella complained. 'Spill the beans, for goodness' sake!'

As the door opened Ava was rolling her eyes in receipt of Bella's pleading look and saying, 'Vito's not my partner or my boyfriend, nor are we involved in anything serious…he's just my lover.'

'Outside the bedroom door I rarely know where I am with your sister!' Vito quipped without batting a single magnificent eyelash while he strolled fluidly across the room to greet her sisters as if it were the most natural thing in the world.

Registering that Vito had heard that unplanned statement, Ava turned a painful beetroot shade, her discomfiture intense. But she hadn't wanted her siblings to get any ambitious ideas about where her relationship with Vito might be heading and a dose of plain speaking had seemed the best approach to take. Ava watched as her siblings reacted predictably to Vito's stunning good looks and white-hot sex appeal. Gina stared at him transfixed while Bella giggled ingratiatingly at almost everything he said. Vito, in comparison, was smooth as silk as he invited her sisters to the Christmas party and asked them about their children. As distanced as though she were on another planet while she had that all-important letter still clutched in her hand, Ava learned that Bella had given birth to a baby boy the previous year, a brother to round out her trio of daughters. Gina, of course, never as child-orientated, still had only one child, a ten-year-old son, and a successful career as a photo-journalist.

Ava was stunned to hear Vito invite her sisters and their husbands to attend the private lunch that was always staged for his closest friends before the party kicked off in the afternoon.

'Why did you do that?' she demanded accusingly when her siblings had gone.

'It seemed polite and you do want your sisters back in your life again, don't you?' Vito asked levelly.

'Sort of...' Too much had happened too fast for Ava to be sure of what she wanted, aside of Vito. He was the one constant she did not need to measure in terms of importance and that hurt as well. How could she have been stupid enough to let her guard down and fall for him again?

'What's wrong?' Vito prompted, watching troubled expressions skim across her expressive face like fast-moving clouds.

Ava explained about the letter.

'Why haven't you opened it yet?'

'I'm afraid to,' she admitted tightly, her blue eyes dark with strain. 'Bella implied it would be disappointing. It's one thing to imagine, something else to actually *see* her words on paper. If it's unpleasant those words will live with me for ever.'

'Maybe I should open it for you...' Vito suggested.

But such a concession to weakness was more than Ava could bear and she slit open the envelope to extract a single piece of lined notepaper adorned with Bella's copperplate script.

Ava,

I'm so sorry, sorrier than you will ever know. I made such a mess of my life and now I've messed up yours as well. I'm sorry I couldn't face visiting you in that place or even seeing you here in hospital—should the authorities have agreed to let you out to visit me. But I couldn't face you. The damage has been done and it's too late for me to do anything about it. I wanted to keep my marriage together—I always put that first and it couldn't have survived what I did at the last. I do love you but even now I'm too scared to tell you the truth—it would make you hate me.

Eyes wet with tears of regret and disappointment for she had had high hopes of what she might find in the letter, Ava pushed the notepaper into Vito's hand. 'It doesn't make any sense at all. I don't know what's she's talking about,' she declared in frustration. 'Gina said Mum was confused and she must have been to dictate that for Bella to write.'

Frowning down at the incomprehensible letter, Vito replaced it in the envelope. 'Obviously your mother felt very guilty about the way she treated you.'

'Did she think I'd hate her when I found out that I wasn't her husband's child?' Her brow furrowed, Ava shook her head, conceding that she would never know for sure what her mother had meant by her words. 'What else could she have meant?'

Vito rested a soothing hand against the slender rigidity of her spine. 'There's no point getting upset about it now, *bella mia*. If your sisters are equally bewildered, there's no way of answering your questions.'

He was always so blasted practical and grounded, Ava reflected ruefully. He didn't suffer from emotional highs or lows or a highly coloured imagination. Reluctant to reveal that she was unable to take such a realistic view of the situation when the woman concerned had been dead for almost eighteen months, Ava said nothing.

His mobile phone rang and he dug it out with an apologetic glance in her direction. That was an improvement, Ava conceded. In the space of little more than a week, Vito had gone from answering constant calls and forgetting her existence while he talked at length to keeping the calls brief and treating them like the interruptions they were. She focused on his bold bronzed profile as he moved restively round the room, another frown drawing his straight black brows together. For once the caller was doing most of the talking, for his responses were brief.

Ava was staring out of the window at the white world of snow-covered trees and lawn stretching into the distance when he finished the call.

'I'm afraid I have to go out,' Vito murmured flatly.

'I'm going to take Harvey for a long walk,' Ava asserted, keen to demonstrate her independence and her lack of need for his presence. It was a downright lie, of course, but it helped to sustain her pride.

CHAPTER TEN

Boxes of decorations littered the big hall. Ava was using a stepladder to dress the tree and cursing the fact that her carefully laid plans were running behind schedule. It had taken most of the day to have the tree felled, brought to the castle and safely erected in the most suitable spot. A towering specimen of uniform graceful shape, the tree looked magnificent, but she had had to search the attics for two hours before she finally tracked down the lights.

Her generous mouth took on an unhappy tilt. After the tragedy of the last Christmas celebrated at the castle three years earlier, all the festive decorations had been bundled away without the usual care and attention and some items had emerged broken while others appeared to have been mislaid. It saddened her to recall that the last time she had dressed a tree Olly had been by her side and in full perfectionist mode as he argued about where every decoration went, adjusted branches and insisted on tweaking everything to obtain the best possible effect. In truth, Olly had adored the festive season as much as Vito loathed it.

To be fair, though, what happy memories could Vito possibly have of Christmas? When he was a boy, his

mother had walked out on his father and him shortly
before Christmas and his father had refused to celebrate
the season in the years that followed. Olly's demise at
the same time of year could only have set the seal on
Vito's aversion to seasonal tinsel. Ava did not want to
be insensitive towards his feelings.

The night before, Vito had fallen into bed beside her
late on and in silence. She did not know where he had
been or what he had been doing and even after she made
it clear that she was still awake he had not offered any
explanation. For the first time as well he hadn't touched
her or reached for her in any way and she had felt ridiculously rejected. Her faith in her insuperable sex appeal
had dive-bombed overnight. She had started wondering
if there was more depth than she knew to his comment
that being with her was 'hard work'. She flinched at that
disturbing recollection. That tabloid story combined
with her distress over her mother's baffling letter and
the emotional mood engendered by her reunion with her
sisters could not have helped to improve that impression. Vito was not accustomed to complex relationships
with women. Perhaps he was getting fed up with all the
problems she had brought into his life and forced him
to share. He might even have reached the conclusion
that he would be quite content to wave goodbye to her
after the party. Last night, she thought painfully, she
had felt as though he had withdrawn from her again,
his reserve kicking back in when it was least welcome.

Her mobile phone rang and she pulled it out of her
pocket.

'It's Vito. I can't make it back for a couple of days
so I'll stay in my apartment. I should mention though
that I've set up a meeting for you with some people

for the day after tomorrow. Will you stay home in the morning?'

'What people? Why? What's going on?' Ava prompted, striving to keep the sound of disappointment out of her response. He was a workaholic—she *knew* he was. He might have worked shorter hours the previous week to be with her but it would be unrealistic to expect that sexual heat and impatience to continue. And to start imagining that maybe another woman had caught his eye or that he wanted a break from the woman he had, perhaps unwisely, invited to stay in his home, was equally reasonable.

'I'm bringing a couple of people I want you to meet,' he advanced.

Her brow furrowed, surprise and curiosity assailing her. 'Do I need to dress up?'

'No. What you wear won't matter,' he said flatly.

Who is it? she was tempted to demand, but she restrained her tongue. Vito already sounded tired and tense and she didn't want to remind him that she could be hard work in a relationship. *Relationship,* get you, she mused irritably as she dug her phone back into her pocket and selected a fine glass angel to hang on the tree with careful fingers. A casual affair was a relationship of sorts but not of the lasting, deep kind that led to commitment. She was with a guy who didn't commit and didn't lie about it either. A whole host of far more beautiful and sophisticated ladies had passed through his life before she came along and not one of them had lasted either. He was thirty-one with neither a marriage nor even a broken engagement under his belt and she was the very first woman to live at the castle with him. At that acknowledgement, her mouth quirked. And what was that concession really worth? She had had nowhere else to stay and it was more convenient for her to organise the party while she lived on the premises.

She checked the rooms set aside for the party. The estate joiner had done a fine job with the Santa grotto for the younger children and the nativity set with life-size figures, which she had hired to place in the opposite corner, added a nice touch about the true meaning of Christmas. The room next door was decorated with a dance theme for the teenagers and rejoiced in a portable floor that lit up. On the day there would be a DJ presiding. Across the hall lay the ballroom where the adult event would take place with a manned bar and music. The caterers had already placed seats and tables down one side and the local florist would soon be arriving to install the festive flower arrangements that Ava had selected.

She found it hard to get to sleep that night even with Harvey sleeping at the foot of the bed. Persuading the dog from his station waiting at the front door for Vito's return had been a challenge. That she could have been tempted to join the dog in his vigil bothered her. It was never cool to be so keen on a man and it would not be long before she betrayed herself and he recognised the fact that she had fallen for him. Then he would feel uncomfortable around her and he wouldn't be able to wait to get rid of her. She would leave after the party with dignity and no big departure scene, she told herself fiercely.

A couple of restless nights in succession ensured that Ava slept in the morning that Vito was bringing company back and she had to wash, dress and breakfast at speed. By the time she heard the helicopter flying in over the roof of the castle, she was pacing in the hall. With a woof of excitement and anticipation, Harvey stationed himself back by the entrance again and Ava suppressed a sigh at the sight.

Vito strode into the castle with three other men, a reality that took Ava aback and she hung back from greeting him. Even so her entire focus was on Vito as she drank in his darkly handsome features and the lithe power of his well-built body sheathed in a dark designer suit.

'Miss Fitzgerald?' A stocky man with a tired but familiar face was smiling at her and extending his hand. 'It's been a long time.'

Ava was stunned: he was the solicitor, Roger Barlow, who had represented her when she was on trial three years earlier.

'Possibly longer for her,' the older blond man behind him quipped, catching her now free hand in his. 'David Lloyd, senior partner with Lloyd and Lloyd Law Associates in London.'

'And this is Gregory James,' Vito introduced the final man in the group, a thickly set balding bearded man, with grave courtesy. 'Gregory and his firm were responsible for upgrading the security on the estate after the break-in we suffered here five years ago.'

Ava nodded, while wondering what all these men had to do with her. Was her solicitor's presence a simple coincidence? She glanced at Vito, belatedly noticing the lines of tension grooving his mouth, the shadows below his eyes. Barely forty-eight hours had passed since she had last seen him and he looked vaguely as if he'd been to hell and back, she thought in dismay, suddenly desperate to know what was going on. Why on earth had he brought members of the legal profession home with him?

Vito suggested they all adjourn to the library where everyone but him took a seat. 'I asked Greg to come here and meet you personally, Ava. He'll explain what this is all about.'

'I saw those photos of you in the newspaper on Sunday,' Greg James volunteered, studying her with calm but curious eyes. 'I read the story and I was very shocked by it. I was at the party here that night as well and I had no idea there had been an accident until I read about it. I left the party an hour before midnight to catch my flight to Brazil where I had my next commission.'

'Greg had no idea you'd been tried and sent to prison for reckless driving because he was working abroad for months afterwards,' Vito explained. 'But after he had read that newspaper he phoned me and suggested we meet up.'

'You weren't the driver that night,' Greg James informed Ava with measured force. 'I saw what happened that evening outside the castle. I thought I was seeing a stupid argument between people I didn't know…with the exception of Vito's brother. I had no idea I was witnessing anything that might be relevant to a court case and I thought no more of it until I learned that you had gone to prison over what happened that night.'

Ava's lips had fallen open and her eyes were wide. Her heart was beating so fast she almost pressed a hand against it because she was feeling slightly dizzy. 'What are you talking about? How could I not have been the driver? And what argument did you see?'

David Lloyd leant forward in his armchair. 'Ava…

your defence at the trial was hampered by the fact that you had no memory of the accident. How could you protect yourself when you remembered nothing?'

'As I said, I left the party early,' Greg continued. 'I'd arranged a taxi pickup and while I was waiting for it on the steps outside I saw an argument take place around a car. There were three people there…you, Vito's brother, Olly, and a large woman in a pink dress.'

'*Three* people,' Ava almost whispered with a frown. 'A large woman?'

'The last thing you remembered before the accident was running down the steps towards Olly's car,' her former solicitor reminded her helpfully.

'The large woman followed you outside and a row broke out between you all,' Greg James supplied. 'That's why I noticed the incident. The lady in the pink dress had obviously had too much to drink. She was very angry and she was shouting all sorts at you and the boy.'

Vito spoke up for the first time. 'I'm sorry but I think the lady in the pink dress was your mother. I also saw her leave the castle in a rush. I assumed she'd had another argument with your father. To my everlasting regret I didn't go outside to check on you and Olly.'

'My…*mother?*' Ava was repeating while studying Vito with incredulity. 'Are you trying to suggest that she was driving?'

'Oh, she was definitely driving that night,' Greg James declared with complete confidence. 'I saw her in the driver's seat and I saw her drive off like a bat out of hell as well.'

Nausea stirred in Ava's tense stomach and she dimly registered that it was the result of more shock than she could handle. She skimmed her strained gaze round the room as if in search of someone who could explain things because her brain refused to understand what she was being told.

'With sufficient new evidence we can appeal your conviction,' David Lloyd informed her seriously. 'My firm specialises in such cases and Vito consulted me for advice yesterday. He didn't want to raise false hopes.'

'Mum couldn't have been there...it's not possible,' Ava whispered shakily. 'It couldn't have been her. I mean, she was banned from driving and she'd stopped drinking.'

'She fell off the wagon again at the party,' Vito countered heavily. 'I can confirm that. I called on Thomas Fitzgerald yesterday and your mother's husband confirmed that he caught your mother drinking that night and that they had a colossal row from which she stormed off saying that she was going home. He assumed she was getting a cab and he was simply relieved she'd left without causing a public scene.'

Ava blinked rapidly and studied her linked hands. Her mother *had* worn a pink dress that night but that surely wasn't acceptable evidence. 'If she was in the car what happened to her after the crash?'

'Obviously she wasn't hurt. We can only assume that she panicked and pulled you into the driver's seat before fleeing home. She would have known that Olly was dead.'

'A woman in a pink dress was seen walking down the road towards the village about the time of the crash.' Roger Barlow spoke up, somewhat shyly, for the first time since his arrival. 'The police did appeal for her to come forward but I'm afraid nobody did.'

'Olly wouldn't have let her drive his car. She wasn't

allowed to drive, she wasn't insured,' Ava mumbled in a daze. She was horrified by the suggestion that her mother had not only abandoned her at the crash site while she was unconscious but had also moved her daughter's body to make it look as though she had been the drunk driver who had run the car off the road into a tree.

'You did try to reason with the woman and so did the boy but she wouldn't listen. She kept on saying that she was sick and tired of people trying to tell her what to do and she repeatedly insisted that she was sober. She was determined to drive and she didn't give Vito's brother a choice about it. She pushed him out of her way and just jumped in the driver's seat and slammed the door. He yanked open the rear passenger door and flung himself in the back seat at the last possible moment and the car went off down the drive like a rocket,' Greg James completed with a shake of his head while he studied Ava's pale shocked face. 'You were the front seat passenger. You weren't driving, you definitely *weren't* driving that car that night…'

'Roger drew my attention to the fact that there were other inconsistencies in your case,' David Lloyd informed her helpfully. 'The police found a woman's footprints in the mud by the driver's door although you were still out cold when the ambulance arrived. One of your legs was also still resting in the foot well of the front passenger seat and the injury to your head was on the left side, suggesting that you had been bashed up against the passenger window.'

'When your mother's husband came home later that night, your mother had locked herself in the spare room and was refusing to answer either the phone or the doorbell,' Vito informed her levelly. 'When did your mother finally come to see you in hospital?'

Ava parted bloodless lips. 'She didn't come to the hospital. She came down with the flu and I was home within a few days and receiving outpatient treatment.'

'And how did she behave when she saw you again?'

'She acted like the accident hadn't happened. She got very upset when…er…Thomas lectured me about how I'd killed Olly and ruined my life.'

'She wasn't upset enough to come forward and admit that she was the driver,' Vito breathed, his tone one of harsh condemnation.

'I think we have a very good chance of, at the very least, having Ava's conviction set aside as unsafe,' David Lloyd forecast with assurance. 'I'm happy to take on the case.'

'And obviously I'll take care of the costs involved,' Vito completed on an audible footnote of satisfaction.

The other men were all heading straight back to London again in the helicopter. As the trio stood chatting together Vito approached Ava, who was still frozen in her armchair showing all the animation of a wax dummy. 'I really do have to get back to the office, *bella mia*,' he imparted, searching her blank eyes with a hint of thwarted masculine frustration. 'I pushed a great deal of work aside to deal with this over the last couple of days. I didn't want to bring it to you without checking out the evidence first.'

'I know…you didn't want to raise false hopes,' she said flatly.

'Naturally all this has come as a shock but say the word and I'll stay if that would make you feel better…'

'Why would it make me feel better?' Ava parted stiff

lips to enquire. 'You've already done more than enough for me. I'll be fine.'

Vito remembered tears running down her face that day in Harrods and silently cursed. Amazon woman didn't need anyone, certainly not him for support. He stepped back, anger glimmering in his stunning dark golden eyes, his strong bone structure taut with self-discipline. 'If you need me, if you have any questions, phone me,' he urged, knowing he wouldn't be holding his breath for that call to come.

'Of course.' Ava looked up at him as if she were trying to memorise his features. In truth she was in so much shock and pain, she felt utterly divorced from him and the struggle to maintain her composure was using up what energy she had left.

As soon as she heard the helicopter overhead again, Ava went and got her coat, collected Harvey from the hall and went outside, her feet crunching over the crisp snow that had frozen overnight.

To Ava, it seemed at that moment as though Vito had unleashed another nightmare into her world. In the same week that Ava had lost the man she had believed was her father, she had been confronted with the horrible threatening image of a mother who might have sacrificed her youngest daughter to save her own skin. Was it true? Ava asked herself wretchedly. Was it true that Gemma Fitzgerald could have done such a thing? Was that what her mother's distraught letter was all about? Gemma's *own* guilt, guilt so great she couldn't even face the prospect of seeing Ava again?

Ava's head was starting to ache with the force of her emotions. She tried to imagine how she would feel without the ever-present burden of feeling responsible for her best friend Olly's death. She *couldn't* imagine it, her own guilt had long since become a part of her. But the pain of thinking that her mother might have stood by doing nothing while her daughter was reviled, tried and sentenced to a long prison term in her place was greater than Ava thought she could stand.

Yet Gregory James had been so sure of facts, so certain of what he had witnessed that night. He *said* that Gemma Fitzgerald had been driving. And his description of the scene he had witnessed before the car set off rang more than one familiar bell for Ava. Her mother had been a forceful personality and, under the influence of alcohol, her temper and her determination to have her own way would have been well-nigh unstoppable. Growing up in such a troubled home, Ava had seen many scenes between her parents that bore out that fact. Few people had been strong enough to stand up to her mother, certainly not kind, always reasonable Olly. Olly wouldn't have known how to handle her mother pushing him away and climbing into his car drunk. He wouldn't have wanted to create a scene. He wouldn't have wanted to hurt or embarrass Ava by calling for help to deal with her obstreperous mother. But he wouldn't have wanted to leave Ava alone in that car either at the mercy of a drunk and angry driver... and that would have been *why* he threw himself into the back seat before her mother drove off and, unhappily, also why he had died.

Ava let the tears overflow and sucked in a shuddering breath in an effort to regain control of her turbulent emotions. Harvey licked at her hand and looked up at her worriedly and she crouched down and hugged him for comfort. She felt so weak and helpless.

What had Vito's motivation been in pushing forward the prospect of trying to clear Ava's name with such zeal? Was it for her sake or...*his own*? Was he more interested in cleaning up her image to ensure that his own remained undamaged? Had he resented the charge that he was sleeping with his brother's killer enough to move heaven and earth to prove that that had not, after all, been the case? She reminded herself that had Gregory James not first contacted Vito, the possibility that she had been unjustly imprisoned would never have occurred to Vito. Just like everyone else he had believed Ava guilty and he had never forgiven her for it...

Her phone rang and she answered it. It was her sister, Bella.

'Are you all right?' Bella asked worriedly.

'Not really,' Ava admitted, swallowing one hiccup only to be betrayed by a second audible one.

'I'll come and pick you up,' Bella told her bossily. 'You shouldn't be dealing with this on your own. Where's Vito?'

'He had to go back to London,' Ava explained, feeling a twinge of guilt at that statement when she recalled his offer to stay. But what would he have stayed for? So that she could weep all over him instead? Prove how much very hard work she could be even in what was supposed to be a fun lightweight affair?

Her sister's home was a former farmhouse on the far side of the village, a cosy home filled with scattered toys, a chubby toddler called Stuart with an enchanting smile and a wall covered with photos of children in school uniform and crayon drawings.

'Excuse the mess,' Bella urged. 'Dad came over last night to talk about this. He's appalled by what Vito had to tell him. To be honest we were all just grateful that Mum disappeared that night without making a big scene. You know what she was like...we assumed she'd caught a cab home. All of us were drinking, none of us were driving. We'd arranged a mini cab for midnight to take us back.'

Ava sipped gratefully at the hot cup of tea Bella had made her. 'Do you think it's true?'

'Well, I always had a problem getting my head round the idea that you could be that stupid and I never could work out why Olly was in the back seat without a seat belt when you were supposedly driving. But in the end we all just assumed you'd gone a bit mad for a few minutes and that few minutes was all it took to wreck your life,' Bella remarked in a pained tone. 'I'm so sorry, Ava.'

'You don't need to be. It's done now. I mean, the police thought I was guilty too.'

'I do remember Mum being really weird about it all,' her sister confided with a grimace of discomfiture. 'Now I can understand why. No wonder she felt guilty. It was an incredibly cruel thing for her to do to you... you not being able to remember the crash delivered you straight into her hands.'

Ava hugged the friendly toddler for security, still freaking out at the belief that her own mother could have taken advantage of her like that.

'I know I shouldn't interfere,' the small blonde woman remarked gingerly, 'but I don't think Vito liked being referred to as your lover in that offhand voice you used.'

'Oh.' Ava went pink. 'I didn't know what else to call him.'

'He's very volatile, isn't he?' Bella murmured reflectively. 'I never saw that in him before. In fact I used to
think he was a bit frozen and removed from all us lesser
mortals, but yesterday it was obvious that he was absolutely raging about what Mum had done to you. I expect
he feels horribly guilty—we all do now.'

'I don't want his guilt,' Ava proclaimed and blew
her nose. 'After the party I'll be going back to London.'

'Oh, Ava, must you?' Bella pressed. 'Gina and I were
looking forward to getting to know you.'

'I would have enjoyed that.' A tremulous smile
formed on Ava's lips as her sister gave her a hug on the
doorstep. 'But I can't hang on Vito's sleeve much longer—it's getting embarrassing.'

Ava returned to the castle. The caterers phoned with
a query and the owner of the firm asked to call out that
afternoon to run through the final arrangements for the
party one last time. Grateful to be occupied, Ava used
her visit as a distraction from her harried thoughts. The
bottom line in her relationship with Vito, she had almost
told her sister, was that he didn't love her. They didn't
have a future together. Vito had not once mentioned
anything beyond the Christmas party and she wasn't
planning to hang around being pathetic in the hope that
he suggested she extend her stay. She would get over
him, it wouldn't be easy but she would manage it. But
the very prospect of a life shorn of Vito tore at her like
a vision of death by a thousand cuts.

Vito phoned at supper time and asked in a worried
tone how she was. His tone set her teeth on edge and
she assured him that she was perfectly all right. He
said he'd probably spend the night at his apartment and
she didn't blame him. He was fed up with all the hassle

and drama she created around her, she decided painfully. She went to bed early, longing for the bliss of sleep, which would settle her tired, troubled mind.

At what point she started dreaming, she later had no clear idea. In her dream she was running down the steps of the castle the night of the crash and she was doing it over and over again. Olly was behind her, telling her he would run her home, and then without the slightest warning the picture in her head changed and her mother erupted into Olly's lecture about Ava's provocative behaviour with Vito.

'I'll drive!' Gemma proclaimed, ignoring Olly before telling him that she was perfectly capable of driving them all home and refused to be driven by a teenager.

As the argument got more heated voices were raised. Ava shouted across the bonnet of the car that Gemma wasn't allowed to drive when she had been drinking and her mother took that as a challenge, thrusting Olly furiously out of her path and jumping into the car to rev the engine like a boy racer. Ava leant across Gemma to try and steal the car keys and the car skidded with squealing tyres on the drive while Olly tried to reason with the older woman and persuade her to stop. The car careened through the gates at the foot of the drive onto the road with Ava screaming at her mother to stop while Olly urged everyone to be calm and think about what they were doing. And a split second later, it seemed, Ava saw the tree trunk looming up through the windscreen, heard Olly cry out her name…and then everything just blanked out.

Ava woke up with a frantic start, her heart hammering, anguish enclosing her like a suffocating cocoon as she realised that she had relived the accident. She was disconcerted to discover that the light was on and Vito, naked but for a pair of jeans, was on his knees beside her. 'You were dreaming and you let out a shriek that would have wakened the dead!' he exclaimed.

But it would never wake Olly, Ava thought foolishly, a sob catching in her throat as she hugged her knees and rocked back and forth. 'I relived the crash…I remember what happened but why now? Why couldn't I remember before?'

'Why would you have wanted to remember it when you thought you were guilty? Was your mother driving?'

Ava nodded jerkily and told him what she had recalled, trembling as she spoke, the images so fresh and frightening she almost felt as though she were trapped back in that car again. In silence, Vito held her close. 'I didn't want you to relive that,' he confessed. 'I didn't really think all this through when I listened to what Greg James had to tell me. I saw what I thought was the chance to fix it all for you and I went and saw David Lloyd and your solicitor and your father to check out all the facts.' His strong profile was tense. 'I was very pleased with myself.'

'Yes,' Ava whispered shakily, glad the tears had stopped, relaxing back into the warmth and security of his arms.

'And then I saw your face this morning and I…I hadn't a clue how to make it better for you,' Vito admitted grudgingly, his frustration over that fact palpable. 'It was only then I saw that you were devastated that your mother could have stood by and hurt you like that.'

'She watched me take her punishment and she never breathed a word,' Ava conceded strickenly. 'Even if she gave way to an impulse to let me take the blame for the crash, she could have thought better of it. She could have made a statement to the police once she realised how ill she was…but even then she didn't think better of what she had done.'

'Let it go. That crash has already ruled your life for far too long,' Vito murmured tautly as he released her and sprang off the bed.

'You weren't sleeping in here with me,' Ava registered with a frown. 'In fact I thought you weren't coming back tonight.'

'I thought better of that but I returned very late and I didn't want to disturb you, *cara mia.*'

'So where are you going now?'

'I left some stuff in my room. I assumed you'd still be up when I got back,' Vito admitted, compressing his lips.

A little less tense, Ava rested back against the pillows. She pushed the jagged images of the crash back out of her mind, still shaken that those mislaid memories had finally broken through to the surface. Her mother had been driving, not her. A sense of relief finally flowed through her but she felt guilty about it, as if somewhere in her mind she still couldn't quite believe that she was entitled to feel that way.

Vito strode back from the door, still bare-chested, his remarkable abs flexing as he settled the items he carried down on the bed in front of her, for all the world like a caveman dragging a dead deer into the cave for his woman.

'Er…you went shopping?' Ava prompted in astonishment, lifting the wilting red roses. 'You should've put these in water to keep them fresh.'

'I haven't physically bought flowers before,' Vito gritted. 'I usually order them on the phone to be delivered.'

'That does cut out the practical aspect,' Ava conceded in an understanding tone, pleased he had chosen her flowers personally. 'Nobody's ever given me flowers before. They're lovely.'

'If they weren't half dead already,' Vito quipped, settling the box of chocolates on her lap.

Ava wasted no time in opening the chocolates while covertly eying the third and final package.

'I'm sorry I didn't appreciate how you would feel about what your mother did to you,' Vito volunteered. 'I couldn't see the wood for the trees.'

'You always think you can fix things.' Ava comfort ate a couple of chocolates and offered them to him before reaching for the final box. It was very light and she peeled off the wrapping and extracted a bubble-wrapped bauble. 'My goodness, it's a tree ornament,' she said, astonished at him having purchased such a festive item.

The hand-decorated bauble twinkled in the light. It was marked with the year. 'Is the date significant?' she asked.

'*Dio mio,* of course it is. It's the year you brought Christmas back to life at Bolderwood. The castle looks fantastic,' Vito informed her, sliding lithely into bed beside her. 'Do you like it?'

'I love it,' she confessed, ensnared by smouldering dark golden eyes and registering that comfort sex was as much on offer as comfort eating.

He removed the tree ornament from her hand and set the chocolates down. But Ava evaded him by scrambling out of bed with the roses. 'I'm just going to soak these in the basin!' she told him, hurrying into the bathroom.

'They're half dead!' Vito growled. 'I'll buy you more tomorrow.'

Ava ran water into the washbasin and caressed a silky petal with an appreciative finger. They were still the very first flowers he'd ever given her and in her opinion, worthy of conservation.

'Thanks for the pressies,' she told him, climbing back into bed. 'I wish I'd got something for you.'

'You're my present,' Vito proclaimed, circling her soft mouth and then ravishing her generous lips with his own with a hunger that made her every sense sizzle with reaction and joy. 'But there's one more I'd like to give you first. It's downstairs below the tree.'

'Oh…downstairs,' Ava responded without enthusiasm, her attention locked to his wide sensual mouth and only slowly skimming up to meet his smouldering dark golden gaze.

'I want you to open it.'

'Now?' Ava pressed in disbelief. 'It's two o'clock in the morning and it's the party tomorrow!'

Vito vaulted off the bed and extended the silk wrap he had bought for her. 'It's important, *bella mia,*' he urged.

With a sigh, Ava got up and slid her arms into the sleeves. 'You can be very demanding.'

'It's not a deal-breaker, is it?' Vito studied her with his shrewd gaze, his innate cunning never more obvious to her and she flushed, wondering how much he had guessed about how she felt about him.

'You let Harvey into your bedroom,' she registered,

hearing the dog whining behind the door at the sound of their voices and letting him out.

Vito seized the opportunity to grab a shirt and put it on. 'He cried at the door.'

They descended the stairs, where the dying fire in the grate was flickering enormous eerie shadows over the walls and the decorations. Ava bent down and switched on the sparkling tree lights before spying the large gift-wrapped box below the huge tree. 'What on earth is it?'

'Your Christmas present.'

'But I wasn't going to *be* here at Christmas!' Ava protested.

'I wouldn't have let you go,' Vito countered stubbornly.

'I was planning to leave the morning after the party,' she reminded him.

His handsome mouth quirked. 'The best-laid plans...' he said.

Ava hauled out the box and began to rip the shimmering golden wrapping paper off it, only to expose another differently wrapped box inside. 'What is this? Pass the parcel?' she teased in surprise.

The pile of discarded wrapping grew larger as the boxes got smaller until finally Ava emerged with one tiny box and paled. 'What is it?'

Vito dropped down on one knee in front of her and asked levelly, 'Will you marry me?'

Ava sucked in air like a drowning swimmer and stared at him with bright blue eyes filled with astonishment. Shock was snaking through her in dizzy waves. 'Where did this idea come from? Are you insane?'

'That's not how you're supposed to respond to a proposal!' Vito pronounced, springing back upright again to gaze down at her with a frown.

Ava opened the box and stared at the gorgeous diamond ring inside, the jewels of which shone with blinding brilliance when the flickering tree lights caught them. She blinked, her throat closing over all tight. 'You don't mean this…you're not thinking about what you're doing. You know you don't want a wife. You know you think that if you get married your wife will divorce you and take your castle and your kids and at least half your money—'

'It's a risk I'm prepared to take to have you in my life,' Vito admitted tautly.

Ava looked up at him with drowning eyes. 'You know, I think that's probably the nicest thing you ever said to me but I *can't* marry you. You're only asking me because you know that I wasn't driving that night, after all,' she condemned painfully. 'And that wouldn't feel right.'

'I bought the ring the day *before* Greg James phoned me,' Vito traded. 'And I can prove it.'

'Before?' Ava pressed, startled by the claim. 'But I thought you couldn't forgive me?'

'And I thought it too until I tried to imagine my life without you,' Vito admitted, crouching down so that they were on the same level, his eyes filled with grave honesty as they met hers. 'The forgiveness was there all along. I just didn't realise that I'd already achieved it. We both loved Olly. He loved you and I love you as well. It's a link we will never lose.'

'You *love* me?' Ava gasped, suddenly out of breath as her heart began to hammer inside her chest.

'Why else do you think I'm asking you to marry me?'

Vito demanded with some impatience. 'I didn't think I would ever fall for anyone but I started falling for you the moment you came back into my life.'

'Oh…' Ava said again, sharply disconcerted. 'I love you too but I thought this was just a casual affair?'

'That was my fault. I'm so used to laying down limits and then you came along and washed them all away. Very quickly, I just wanted you, *amata mia.*' Vito reached for her hand, tugged the ring from the box and threaded it onto her engagement finger. 'And tomorrow, when you're acting as hostess at the party, I want that ring on your finger so that everyone appreciates that you're the woman I intend to marry.'

Ava looked down at the ring sparkling on her finger in wonderment and then back at him to take in the tenderness in his gaze with a leaping joyful sense of recognition. 'You really do love me…even though I'm hard work?'

'You made me think, you made me try to be something more than I was. No woman ever affected me that way before,' Vito confided. 'You're not hard work… you're the best thing that ever happened to me. Only one thing about you bothers me…'

Concern assailed Ava. 'What?'

'You don't confide in me. You spent three years in prison and you never ever talk about it.'

'It's not something you want to accidentally refer to in the wrong company. It was a different world with its own set of rules,' Ava told him uncomfortably. 'I had some very low moments in prison. I was scared a lot of the time. I got bullied for having a posh accent. I was strip-searched once because my cellmate was caught with drugs. At the beginning I was on suicide watch under constant surveillance for weeks—'

Troubled, Vito gripped her hand. 'You were suicidal?'

'No, I never was. Unfortunately the psychologist thought I was more at risk. But I was down because I got a six-year sentence for drunk driving. I had no visitors, nothing to do, it took me a long time to adapt and learn how to keep myself occupied.'

'How did you adapt?'

She told him about the reading and writing programme she had eventually participated in and how feeling useful had lifted her mood. The move to an open prison where she had fewer restrictions had also provided a tremendous boost.

'When my parole was granted, when I knew I was getting out, I decided to put the whole experience behind me,' she admitted. 'I didn't want it colouring my life for ever. I just wanted to forget it…can you understand that? Remembering those years just made me feel bad about myself.'

'I do understand,' Vito murmured tautly, closing his hand over hers in reassurance.

Ava shivered. 'It's cold. Let's go back to bed.'

Vito bent down and scooped her up in his arms.

'You can't carry me up the stairs!' Ava told him.

But he did, although he was noticeably relieved to settle her down on the bed again.

Ava dealt him a teasing smile. 'You're wrecked. You'll not be fit for anything now.'

Vito laughed appreciatively as he unzipped his jeans. '*Dio mio,* I love you! Do you realise I've never said those words to anyone before?'

'Not even when you were a teenager?'

'I was a very cynical teenager. Watching my father screw up after my mother left him made a big impression on me. My father thought he was in love with every new woman who came into his life and then, five minutes later, it would all be over again,' he explained with a curled lip. 'I didn't think I had what it took to fall in love and then you came along and lit up everything for me like the sun on a dull day.'

'You do realise that marrying me will commit you to celebrating Christmas every year?' Ava warned him.

'I'll share it with you. I'll always remember that Christmas first brought us together. We'll make new memories. I feel I can be myself with you.'

'Domineering, arrogant, impatient, stubborn,' Ava slotted in, spreading her fingers across his hair-roughened chest and gazing into black-fringed dark golden eyes that made her heart quicken its pace. 'But I do love you very very much. You are also generous and kind and surprisingly thoughtful.'

Vito lifted his tousled dark head in apparent wonderment. 'Is that a compliment from you?'

'I'll give you the occasional one,' Ava promised, running possessive fingers through his black silky hair and studying him. 'You always felt like mine and now you are finally…'

He kissed her and her head swam. She muttered something about needing all her sleep with the party ahead: he ignored it. In the end she kissed him back and the excitement sizzling between them took over to send them soaring with the passion their deep emotions had generated. Afterwards, Ava could never recall feeling happier or more secure and she could feel the past sliding back into its proper place. She had learned lessons from that past but she wanted her future fresh and free of regrets.

The next day the party was an amazing success. Ava wore the green velvet dress under protest, thinking it was far too fancy. Many of the guests arrived on coaches laid on by their employer. She presided as hostess over a select lunch and her ring was very much admired. Vito talked of a winter wedding, Ava gave him a look and talked of a summer one and asked her sisters to be bridesmaids.

'You might be pregnant,' Vito breathed when he got her alone again.

'Of course I'm not. Is that why you asked me to marry you?' Ava asked worriedly.

'Of course not. I'm marrying you because I can't live without you, you little minx,' Vito groaned. 'I suppose I could wait until Easter?'

'No, I'll be a summer bride. We've got to be engaged at least six months to prove that we can live together,' she told him seriously.

'Of course we can. The summer's too far away.'

They got married at Easter and she wasn't pregnant. Vito admitted to being disappointed by that discovery and the idea of a baby took root. The idea of making a family gave Ava a warm, secure feeling inside.

'I don't think it's possible to love anyone more than I love you,' Vito told her on their wedding night in Hawaii.

And Ava knew she felt the same way and rejoiced in the fact that they could agree on some things.

EPILOGUE

OLIVIA Barbieri was born after a short labour two years later, forcing her mother to ask for her recently won place at medical school to be deferred. She had her mother's eyes and her father's hair and even as a baby proved to be rather fond of getting her own way.

Vito grew accustomed to being engulfed by dogs, child and wife when he came home and discovered much to his own surprise that he loved it. His castle had finally become a home. Harvey had been joined by Freda, a cross terrier puppy tied up with string to the gates and abandoned one evening. Vito had put up less of a fight to that development than expected but the dogs slept downstairs in what used to be the boot room. From an early age Olivia displayed every sign of wanting to sleep there as well and had to be strenuously reclaimed from her doggy companions. Ava had also become fast friends with her sisters and the three families regularly met up together.

Three years after their marriage, Ava commenced studying medicine. She had thought long and hard before reapplying to medical school but had come to the conclusion that she needed a strong career to focus on for the future. She knew it would be difficult to study and do work placements in hospitals at the same time as she had a young child but Vito was prepared to reduce his hours and work more from home so that he could be around to step into the breach. That same year, Ava had her conviction for drunk driving set aside as unsafe and she was content with that judgement.

On their fourth anniversary, Vito treated Ava to a second honeymoon in Tuscany although this time their daughter and her nanny came as well. Long lazy days in the sunlight provided a welcome break from their mutually busy schedules. Even before they flew home, Ava suspected that she was pregnant again and she was pleased for she wanted her children to be close enough in age to play together.

'I'm delighted but I had assumed we were only having one child, *bella mia,*' Vito confided, wondering if he would ever get over the suspicion that he had put a wedding ring on a whirlwind.

'But you're pleased?' Ava wrapped her arms round him, thinking that he was still the most gorgeous guy she had ever met.

'Of course I am. I love you, I love Olivia and I'll love the new baby as well,' Vito forecast with a grin. 'My life just keeps on getting better and better.'

'Do you think another dog would enrich your life too?' Ava asked, quick as a flash to take advantage of the right moment. 'Marge has a nice little—'

'I'll think about it. Don't force my hand,' Vito warned his wife.

'Of course not.'

'And don't look so sad. You know I can't stand it when you look sad,' Vito groaned in despair.

'I love you so much, Vito,' Ava confided. 'I knew you wouldn't say no!'

* * * * *

Mills & Boon® Hardback
September 2012

ROMANCE

Unlocking her Innocence	Lynne Graham
Santiago's Command	Kim Lawrence
His Reputation Precedes Him	Carole Mortimer
The Price of Retribution	Sara Craven
Just One Last Night	Helen Brooks
The Greek's Acquisition	Chantelle Shaw
The Husband She Never Knew	Kate Hewitt
When Only Diamonds Will Do	Lindsay Armstrong
The Couple Behind the Headlines	Lucy King
The Best Mistake of Her Life	Aimee Carson
The Valtieri Baby	Caroline Anderson
Slow Dance with the Sheriff	Nikki Logan
Bella's Impossible Boss	Michelle Douglas
The Tycoon's Secret Daughter	Susan Meier
She's So Over Him	Joss Wood
Return of the Last McKenna	Shirley Jump
Once a Playboy...	Kate Hardy
Challenging the Nurse's Rules	Janice Lynn

MEDICAL

Her Motherhood Wish	Anne Fraser
A Bond Between Strangers	Scarlet Wilson
The Sheikh and the Surrogate Mum	Meredith Webber
Tamed by her Brooding Boss	Joanna Neil

0812 GEN STD HB

Mills & Boon® Large Print
September 2012

ROMANCE

A Vow of Obligation	Lynne Graham
Defying Drakon	Carole Mortimer
Playing the Greek's Game	Sharon Kendrick
One Night in Paradise	Maisey Yates
Valtieri's Bride	Caroline Anderson
The Nanny Who Kissed Her Boss	Barbara McMahon
Falling for Mr Mysterious	Barbara Hannay
The Last Woman He'd Ever Date	Liz Fielding
His Majesty's Mistake	Jane Porter
Duty and the Beast	Trish Morey
The Darkest of Secrets	Kate Hewitt

HISTORICAL

Lady Priscilla's Shameful Secret	Christine Merrill
Rake with a Frozen Heart	Marguerite Kaye
Miss Cameron's Fall from Grace	Helen Dickson
Society's Most Scandalous Rake	Isabelle Goddard
The Taming of the Rogue	Amanda McCabe

MEDICAL

Falling for the Sheikh She Shouldn't	Fiona McArthur
Dr Cinderella's Midnight Fling	Kate Hardy
Brought Together by Baby	Margaret McDonagh
One Month to Become a Mum	Louisa George
Sydney Harbour Hospital: Luca's Bad Girl	Amy Andrews
The Firebrand Who Unlocked His Heart	Anne Fraser

0812 GEN STD LP

Mills & Boon® Hardback

October 2012

ROMANCE

Banished to the Harem	Carol Marinelli
Not Just the Greek's Wife	Lucy Monroe
A Delicious Deception	Elizabeth Power
Painted the Other Woman	Julia James
A Game of Vows	Maisey Yates
A Devil in Disguise	Caitlin Crews
Revelations of the Night Before	Lynn Raye Harris
Defying her Desert Duty	Annie West
The Wedding Must Go On	Robyn Grady
The Devil and the Deep	Amy Andrews
Taming the Brooding Cattleman	Marion Lennox
The Rancher's Unexpected Family	Myrna Mackenzie
Single Dad's Holiday Wedding	Patricia Thayer
Nanny for the Millionaire's Twins	Susan Meier
Truth-Or-Date.com	Nina Harrington
Wedding Date with Mr Wrong	Nicola Marsh
The Family Who Made Him Whole	Jennifer Taylor
The Doctor Meets Her Match	Annie Claydon

MEDICAL

A Socialite's Christmas Wish	Lucy Clark
Redeeming Dr Riccardi	Leah Martyn
The Doctor's Lost-and-Found Heart	Dianne Drake
The Man Who Wouldn't Marry	Tina Beckett

Mills & Boon® Large Print

October 2012

ROMANCE

A Secret Disgrace	Penny Jordan
The Dark Side of Desire	Julia James
The Forbidden Ferrara	Sarah Morgan
The Truth Behind his Touch	Cathy Williams
Plain Jane in the Spotlight	Lucy Gordon
Battle for the Soldier's Heart	Cara Colter
The Navy SEAL's Bride	Soraya Lane
My Greek Island Fling	Nina Harrington
Enemies at the Altar	Melanie Milburne
In the Italian's Sights	Helen Brooks
In Defiance of Duty	Caitlin Crews

HISTORICAL

The Duchess Hunt	Elizabeth Beacon
Marriage of Mercy	Carla Kelly
Unbuttoning Miss Hardwick	Deb Marlowe
Chained to the Barbarian	Carol Townend
My Fair Concubine	Jeannie Lin

MEDICAL

Georgie's Big Greek Wedding?	Emily Forbes
The Nurse's Not-So-Secret Scandal	Wendy S. Marcus
Dr Right All Along	Joanna Neil
Summer With A French Surgeon	Margaret Barker
Sydney Harbour Hospital: Tom's Redemption	Fiona Lowe
Doctor on Her Doorstep	Annie Claydon

0912 GEN STD LP